Divergent Lives of No Consequence:
Short Stories

By:

Juan J Alemán II

"Life is merely a series of events that leads to death."

Table of Contents:

Foreword:

Many times, as you sit and think about the world, you have rational thoughts about the state we are in and where we are headed. The following stories are somewhat fantastical and irrational. You may become angry, sad, shocked, or, heaven forbid, triggered at what you read. And that is okay. My stories are for those that think the world is not exactly perfect and that is quite all right. It's what we make of it.

The characters are not intended to reflect anyone that has ever existed or may ever exist, but a lot of them are pieces of me. In writing, I believe that the best characters live somewhere inside the author's existence and have had some impact on their life.

Am I any one of my characters, or do I even espouse the ideas that I write? Don't focus on that. Focus on the tangible aspects of the stories. Everyone has pain, anger, and sadness. Most feel superior, entitled, or better than others. And few are homicidal, megalomaniacs, or suicidal. But this book deals with people that exhibit all of those (and other) traits. I say this not to induce the weak to walk away or the curious to begin tearing through the book. My actual intention is to not catch the reader by surprise. And if you are in need of it, there are plenty of triggers within the following pages.

My book is a summary of things done, seen, thought, and breathed into life. Enjoy what you can and experience the rest.

"If you can't be free in your mind, then you are truly in a cage."

-Juan Aleman II (Puyallup, WA; February 2025)

Youth:

The Boy

The boy, a fireplug of a young man. He's short for his age and has obviously struggled with weight. A Mexican boy in a small town in the South, it was a daily struggle. Every face around him at school was black or white; having no one that looks like you can be scary, but he took it in stride. He barely spoke English when he first started school here, and the English that he did know he had learned from TV. A few years on, he spoke perfect English, but everyone was friends by then and it was too late to become one of them. The funny thing about a Mexican kid that speaks perfect English at a young age—they don't speak Spanish that well. The English speakers don't like you because you don't look like them, and your own family won't like you because you don't speak Spanish like they do. The double-edged sword of being an outsider everywhere you go.

He walks slowly down the sidewalk, diligently

attempting to step on each crack in the sidewalk. His mother had angered him again; he wanted to hedge his bets and make sure her back was good and broken before he got home. As a child, you never really know how cruel some of the things are that you believe, the sayings that are passed forward, the ways people speak to one another. It's all truly vile. But it's what developing minds do: they make up mean rules to live by, and a caste system begins with no knowledge of what is happening.

He walks ahead, and just thinking of his mother brings up a well of emotions. He pictures her yellow, parchment-like, saggy, veiny skin. Even at 12 and being short himself, he's a bit taller than the junkie he calls Mom. She's rail thin. Most of the boyfriends she brings into the house give her the money she needs to get drugs. And the others, they just straight up give her drugs to get the night with her. He'd never met his father; for all he knew, it was probably one of guys that spent the night from time to time.

Sure, many things are learned at home: hate, racism, and a healthy fear of your parents' hands. But, quite naturally, kids come up with ideas of hierarchy amongst one another.

Interestingly, it's based on looks, size, and dress. And our boy has no looks, he's oversized, and most of his clothes are from the local Goodwill. But it is what it is.

The boy kicks small rocks from the sidewalk into the roadway. He doesn't seem to care if he hits a person or a car. He is angry again; Mom treats him poorly. She hits him on every occasion that she sees fit. Most days, he really doesn't care anymore—sure, it hurts, but only for a while. They can only physically hurt you so much.

Hurt. Yeah, slaps and punches, they hurt. But the real hurt though, that's the words. The mean words, they hurt the boy more than anything else. He knows he's fat, he knows he's ugly, he knows he's stupid… He knows all of it! She reminds him daily and he's tired. He's 12 and he hates living. He hates school, and nobody likes him there. He's near tears as he realizes that he hates himself. Some people would find it strange for a child to hate themselves. It's difficult to explain self-hate to those that can look in the mirror and be happy, those that can look to their friends for support, to be built up. For those with a home like the boy, one filled with non-stop ridicule, anger, and pain— yeah, self-hate is easy. Even now, adults wonder, what do kids know about hate? Kids' lives are all cartoons, snacks, and homework.

The boy's tears burn his cheeks. He knows hate. He wipes the tears; he hates crying. All the men that spend the night, they call him a pussy when they hear him crying in his room. Some of those men had given him very bad reasons to cry, once they got bored with Mom. He grows angrier and sadder with each step. He thinks, *Fuck those people that don't know or understand what kids can feel or not feel! And fuck those men that like kids.* He begins to cry even harder.

He wonders if there is a God. *If there is, why does he hate me? Why did I get the mother I got?* And the big question, the one that he falls asleep to and wakes up to: *If I just "accidentally" stepped into the road in front of a car…would He know?*

It's not killing yourself if you step in front of a car by accident. Even if you cause the accident, right? For all he knew, and it wasn't much, just a couple shows talking about suicide— that was the word, suicide? Anyway, accidents happen. And you don't go to hell for an accident, right? Then, in a fresh wave of anger, the boy thinks, *What does it even matter?* He is already in hell.

The sun has begun to wane in the distance and the boy is not aware of where he might be. He has been walking since having the taste knocked out of his mouth this morning. Some days he got a reason for getting smacked around; today, he just caught a stiff hand. The blood that came from his mouth tasted like a penny. He thought it was funny that something that came out of you would taste like money.

The boy looks up and realizes he's headed toward the lake. He likes the lake; it wouldn't be hard to find a place to sleep because there are empty cabins all over the place. He knows that his mother won't miss him; she's busy at night. He'd heard some of the guys that came over at night call her a good whore. He didn't really know what it meant, but he'd heard it on TV. So, for that reason, she wouldn't miss him until she got done with her job and woke up from her high the next morning.

The things in life that make it worth living as a kid are simple. A kid shouldn't have to deal with a parent's vices. Between the drugs, men coming in and out, and liking to slap the boy around, this boy's life has been difficult. He's no stranger to the lake cabins. Most of the time, the cabins were completely empty. Sometimes there were others that were hiding out, mostly junkies and drifters, and just like for the boy, the cabins were a perfect hideout.

Many nights in those cabins, the boy had run into older people. Some were men and some were women, but they all treated him well. No matter that they were considered bottom of the barrel people; they didn't mess with the kid they called Paco. In fact, they treated him better than his mother. They listened to his outlandish and childish stories, they taught him that drinking and drugs were fun but were ultimately a dead end. A lot of those people, mostly the drifters, would caution him against the drugs. The people that he met that had abused drugs but were now trying to start over, they told him that it's not a good life. It was the "Stay in school and just say no!" type speeches that kept him straight. That, and knowing what it had done to his mother.

Sure, some of the junkies had shared some of their booze and weed with him. It was rare, and it didn't even taste good to him. Most of those people weren't what you expected when you thought of the homeless or vagrants, they were the lost. Keeping a boy like Paco off the streets, off drugs, and safe was something they took personally.

The boy hoped he might run into one of his friends tonight. He really wasn't that angry anymore, and as he calmed, he began to feel the weight of the day, which led to him being sad and lonely. Just lonely. Loneliness is the devil to a child. That beast will lead you down a dark path, and quickly. When the boy was alone, he did things he shouldn't. All kids do unspeakable things when they're alone…at least, that's what the boy thought in those moments. He never thought of them around others. His entire life, he'd thought that people could see your thoughts. The boy believed some strange things: people on the TV could see you, people around you could see your thoughts, and the worst was when he was in the bathroom—nothing with eyes could be in there with him…nothing, because the pictures with eyes saw him as well.

The boy hadn't looked in many windows, but he didn't see any of his friends. So tonight, he would end up in a cabin alone for the night. It would be cold, and he would lay in the dark wishing he could just be happy for once. At twelve, he had cried many more tears than any child should. Lonely nights, long days, and sadness were his life.

He's tired but can't sleep. The boy stares into the darkness. It makes him think of a song he had heard his mother listen to when she was coming down; it just said something like, hello to the darkness. Yeah, he loved the idea of that line. He feels those words every time he's alone in the dark.

He had learned from the world what other children would find out as adults, and the childlike things he knew were either guesses or things he'd seen on TV. He'd never had a mother or father's attention to learn those things. In rural country towns, there aren't gangs; instead, there's just bad kids and good kids. He was already one of the bad ones, and that would never change while he was in this shitty little town. Nothing he did would ever change the fact that he was a bad kid. There are no second chances when your whole world—the world you know and that thinks it knows you—has judged you. Even when you get older, you can only be whatever they decided you were all those years ago.

Wasting time—that's what he's doing with his life. And it will never change as long as he's here. The boy looks around the room and settles on a dirty patch of floor that has some old dirty blankets. He thinks to himself, again, that he's a waste. Not a waste of time, but a waste of a life. It's quite funny that everyone around him—people that would never know him, didn't care to know him—would just make up stories. They're just as bad as him, right? They're judging him on who his mother is, or what they may have thought they heard. But mostly, it's things they just made up.

"Did you hear?"

The boy heard that most of the time he walked by a crowd of his so-called peers. It sucked getting treated poorly at home; it was bad. But in public, he felt it was even worse. It was one thing to take shit from his mother. She wielded her power over him with an iron fist, a leather belt, and, at times, a frying pan. He felt that the harder the item she hit him with, the better she felt about it. At least she looked happier when she left him on the ground.

He just feels empty inside. But the school, his classmates and peers, and all the people that live in this town do not deserve that power.

More than once, he had been dragged off by some unsuspecting jerks that thought he wouldn't defend himself. That theory went away quickly. Two successful fights can make anything disappear, but not everyone buys in, and some still try to push. Typically, it started with names, moved to shoves, and eventually he was being grabbed by campus security. It was unfair; he knew the kids didn't like him, but what crushed him was that the teachers and staff didn't like him either.

Adults think they can cover their disdain for a child. Note to adults: Most kids aren't as stupid as you think they are. They see and sense how you feel. Educators should not have favorites, but they do. The teachers in this sleepy little town are just like the kids they're teaching: small minds, small dreams, no sense of direction. It's said that "those who can't… teach." The boy thought, *I may never be much, but I'll leave here and be better than anyone in this town can imagine.* He didn't want or need to impress anyone, but he wanted to prove something to himself. He's not garbage. He's not meant to just disappear into the waves of faceless crowds. He will do something with his life. Even if it's dying by accidentally stepping into the road one day.

He had long since drifted to sleep in that dingy room on a small bunch of dirty blankets on the cold hard floor. The boy had fallen asleep thinking his negative and unhappy thoughts. But he rested quite peacefully knowing that he would not be bothered by anyone—the guests in the other cabins, and even in the other rooms of this cabin, would look after him. It's funny how the people that are considered the dregs of society have a stronger moral compass than the righteous upstanding citizens. Right now, he didn't know it, but later in life, he would fondly remember these people as his real family. In a small town, you don't see the homeless. Homelessness is a big-city problem. What you have in little towns are people that walk the streets during the day and find shelter in the evenings. No muss, no fuss, and no homeless people to run the tourists away. Yes, even little towns with their bed and breakfasts, antique stores, and art & wine walks bring in tourists.

It's a colder night than the boy had anticipated; he woke up stiff and wishing he had found more blankets. Instead, he was freezing and ready to warm up. He gets up, walks toward his home, and hopes to the heavens that his mother is still passed out from last night's activities.

He steps into a littered and smelly living room. It briefly crosses his mind that he'll end up cleaning the area later today. Being the janitor is his penance for being born to this cruel woman. Yes, the janitor, waste, sometimes victim, and resident punching bag.

He lays down, pulls a handful of dirty blankets up to his chin, and kicks his feet up to get the lower end of the blankets to tightly wrap under his feet. He loves feeling the blankets suck him in (especially on mornings that start out this cold). Then he drifts off again. When his mother wakes up, it will all start over again. But for now, he'll drift off like a child with no cares, no fears, and no hidden bruises.

These dreams, today's dreams, are about the father who

he never met. How different would the world be if his father knew about him? Maybe he would want to be with the boy, just like the boy wanted to be with him. It's amazing the dreams that fill a child's mind. The person that ran away and had never met nor knew this boy, well, that person became a de facto hero.

Why?

He was a hero because he had never hurt the child. If he had been there, he would stop all the pain. Wouldn't he? The question lingers in the mind of a child. When all you know is bad, any change must be good. Sure, things would be so much better had he stayed around to be a dad. Boys need a father, don't they? If he had been a good boy, if he had done something different, his dad might have come and taken him away from this place. Maybe he had met his father, and seeing this fat, squatty piece of lard had made him leave without saying a word.

The boy grew angry from time to time as a kid. And as he got older, he had gotten bigger than his mother. He was thinning out a bit. He was still ugly, and time couldn't change that. But his life had not changed for the better. If only Dad would have saved him… Right?

After he woke, the boy recalled a heated argument. One of the many men that floated in and out of the house had slapped the taste out of the boy's mouth. It took a few minutes to get his hearing and his bearings back. In a moment of horror and anger, he yelled at his mother for what had happened. He told her that he was tired of getting slapped around by her men. He was 10 at the time. He told her how he couldn't take it anymore. How he wanted to go live with his father.

What followed was the most painful few minutes of his young life. Even now, thinking of what she had told him broke his heart.

"First of all, don't you fucking talk to me like that, you fat little bastard!" his mother began, ending with a healthy slap to make sure she had his attention. "I have these men here to take care of me, and you are always sticking your head in where it don't belong."

He stood there breathing heavily, his anger continued to be spurred on by the taste of blood that lingered in his mouth. He was on the verge of tears. It's something to behold as a pre-teen when you most want to be angry, tears begin to flow. You can't stop them. And the angrier you become, the more they just flow. Like lava flowing over his cheeks, the tears stung, but not as much as what happened next. He'd played this sentence over and over in his head. No two ways about it, she said it to hurt him and it would never go away.

She turned away from the boy, to go back to her man of the hour. But she looked back for a brief moment and said, "And your father doesn't want you either, so you will stay here and like it!"

Either! That was the word that had stung. That was his reality. His hero, his dad, the man that would walk through fire for him—the boy now realized that all those things were parts of a story he had made up in his head and kept telling himself over and over. No one was coming for him. Not today, not ever. And the bitch of it all? His mother didn't want him "either." Maybe, just maybe, she didn't mean it exactly that way. But he knew better. She had meant what she said. As a child, you hear everything. You see everything. Children are impressionable, and as far as the boy is concerned, what he knows of life is, "No one wants me."

So, he lies staring at the ceiling, wanting sleep, but it eludes him again. He wonders what becomes of a person when there is no love in their life. Sure, he'd always go home after a night in one of the cabins. And he'd live with his mother till he aged out of school or graduated, whichever happened first. But right now, he lies there thinking of the future. A future where he loves himself, where he is happy, where his mother no longer bothers him or needs him for food stamps, WIC, or free rent.

Many people think that when you have a depressing childhood, you immediately think of killing yourself. It's a teenage thing, right? Wrong! Not everyone sees that as an inevitable end. The boy sees leaving, making his way far from this town, and making a life for himself as the only way to salvage the shit he had as a kid.

The truth to it all is that for all the dirty clothes, his

smell, his greasy face and hair, and his shabbiness, the boy feels that he could do better alone. What you are as a child is not always what you become as an adult. He didn't want to be a popular, cool, or even handsome man. He wanted to be…happy.

He chased happiness daily, but his life right now would never let him reach that happiness. Not until he left this place, left it in his rearview.

He had dozed off, but he still feels cold. Even with his blankets firmly wrapped under his feet, the cold has worked its way through. He is awakened by the sunrise and the bright warmth that pours in through the dirty window. The boy wakes up before anyone else stirs. He checks on his mother; she's half-covered and her pale, bruised skin looks grey this morning. The man, he doesn't recognize; he must be a new customer. He walks slowly away from the bedroom and out the front door. He'll wander the neighborhood and the sleepy town for as long as he can. He doesn't really want to arrive back home. He knows two things: she doesn't want him there, and a beating is waiting once she wakes up. But truthfully, he no longer cares.

The boy doesn't know the word epiphany, but he has one in those moments of walking the streets that morning. He clearly sees where he will be in ten to fifteen years. Clean, tall, well spoken, someone that is respected. He'll get help with the bad thoughts: the sadness, the nonsensical thoughts of pictures and videos seeing him and reading his thoughts. Time spent with therapists would heal him. Once healed, he would become even stronger.

Next, he would come back here for her funeral. She got a bad batch and died with a dirty needle hanging out of her arm; the john for the night that gave her the dope was long gone. She had laid there for weeks before the smell was finally enough to bring the police for a welfare check. There is no will, no one else will attend, and unless he forks out the money, she will end up in the potter's field.

He will walk the road from the housing project where he grew up toward the lake where he spent many nights away from the molesters and dope fiends that were his mother's "friends." The boy will stare at the old school where he attended oh so many years ago. The school will have been abandoned for years; it was shabby when he was there as a kid. The overgrown grass, the moss circling the buildings, and the vines of ivy covering the walls will make him wonder if time has aged him as much as it has these old buildings. He'll rub his face and forehead, searching for wrinkles that show age, but he won't find any just yet. He'll stand there and look upon the images of what the town has become with the eyes of a man that has seen what the world has to offer outside the city limits. He'll walk to the lake, where he spent so many of his developing days. The buildings there will be unkempt, old, and creaky. The boy will see that time has had its way with all that he knew as he grew up. The people, the land, and the surroundings would be a speck on a map now. This was the type of place that people went to disappear. It was clear now: if you stay here, your mind dies a slow, painful death—just like everything here.

There he would be, on the edge of the lake. He would think to himself, *"Did I ever actually go swimming? Or even walk past those cabins at the far end of the lake?"*

He'd grin and remove his shoes and socks, roll up his pant legs, and feel the water for the first time…

The boy does not know where he is, but he pauses from his walk home. He's 12 again, and he decides not to wait to come back many years from now and try the water. The boy walks toward the water, past the cabins, and wonders what comes next as he wades into the chilly water and looks around the woods surrounding the lake.

He'd seen a show on TV about making money by selling some stuff. There had been a man in a powder-blue suit; he had a receding hairline with a greasy comb-over of greying hair, and he wore these sunglasses, and it all looked like a beach, but fake. And this shyster finished his pitch with, "Life is what you make of it."

The boy loved that; life is what you make of it. To him, it meant that you can be from nowhere, be an only child and a punching bag for a shitty parent, and you can let it make you a victim. Or you can learn how to live your best life, because life is what you make of it.

As he steps through the cold morning fog coming from

the woods and onto the lake, it strikes him as funny. The boy had changed his perspective by seeing what he wanted to be, and he didn't yet know how to get there, but at least he'd seen himself there.

In that moment, he knows that what he had seen as a future was only one outcome of many that are possible for him. He will not be a victim. He will not let the world run over him. He will change his outcome.

The boy in those quiet moments of that morning realizes that he controls his life. If he controls nothing else, he controls his outcome. There is no fate, no overreaching arc that life must take. It's choices, actions, and words that make us what we are and what we can be—our circumstances are merely challenges to finding out who we really are.

He can no longer feel his feet, the water is freezing

cold. He giggles at the idea of having stepped in the lake ahead of schedule. The boy uses some old material he sees on the ground to dry his feet. He puts on his socks, slips on his shoes, and stands to dust himself off and heads home.

The boy walks with a new sense of purpose. It won't always be this world that he's in now. Seeing it, smelling it, and feeling it are strides toward being that person. He is renewed by his discoveries and the opportunities that lie ahead. The boy knows his life has purpose. It doesn't matter where you come from, what you've seen and dealt with in life; all you need is hope. All children need at least that—hope. If you believe it can be better, make it just that.

The boy decides that if you give up, then, yes, it's over. The important thing is to not give up. The boy had once read a book where climbers had tried to get to the top of Mt. Everest and even the best of them found difficulties. It was a virtual graveyard of elite climbers a mere few hundred yards or less from the top. And none of those people, none of them, had given up. They literally climbed till they died. No matter how well prepared you are, sometimes you will fail. That did scare him, but he remembers the one thing that will be his calling card for the remainder of his life: Life is what you make of it.

Service:

The Veteran—
Or How the World Can No Longer Understand Me

He sits in the lobby. He waits and hates looking at the scum that fills this shithole. Then he wonders for a moment, *Am I scum?*

As a child, Diego had been a big fan of his grandfather. Grandpa Mike was a veteran. He had lost part of his leg in World War II. Diego spent days during his summers at his grandparents' home, looking at pictures from the war. His grandfather had been a sight in his uniform. It was those images that made Diego want to be a soldier; imagining himself serving his country and getting to be the man in a uniform.

"Thank you for your service." That was Diego's favorite phrase when someone had seen him in uniform…when he had still been active duty. Now, all that was over. Now he's in this lobby, looking at everyone here, and the thought hits his mind again. *Am I scum?*

The thought angers him even more. He begins to sweat a bit. He remembers being overseas, how simple life was. You kill or you are killed. That was it. The law of the jungle. The simplicity of it all… That is what he loved about the military. Now that he's out; well, no more respect for "Sarge."

"Sanchez, Diego… Sanchez!" The voice fills the lobby and stops his thoughts—for a brief moment.

"Moving!" he responds. That never changes. The Army gave him that little saying; let them know you've heard and you are on the way.

"Mr. Diego Sanchez?" the short lady standing in the doorway says impatiently. She looks like she has been doing this for a short time. Diego guesses that she probably finished college two to three years ago. A kid. A fucking kid with a college degree. She looks like one of those sorority girls that parties every weekend and went to college for an "MRS" degree. He doesn't like her tight clothes; *not professional*, he thinks to himself, *and she is wearing too much perfume*. He follows closely, then realizes that she had called him *Mr. Sanchez*.

Mister? No one calls a soldier *Mister*. "But you aren't a soldier anymore, are you, old man?" Diego tells himself.

With a bit of a growl, "Yes, ma'am! Diego Sanchez right here."

"Hello, Mr. Sanchez! Please, come on back with me." They begin to walk toward her desk. "My name is Valerie Jenkins. It's a pleasure to meet you.

Looks like a beautiful day out there."

Small talk, he thinks to himself. Why does he even have to be in here with that kid? He absent-mindedly replies with his own small talk. As he speaks, he thinks of this bubble-headed blonde drunk in the sorority house. He stares blankly at her for a moment; he's lost. His gaze is beginning to take in the room. His reality is that he is sizing up the room. Who would be a challenge in a fight? Who is carrying any kind of weapons? Where are the exit points? A soldier, for the remainder of their life, should they make it back home, spends time sizing up common areas where there are possible threats. He can't speak for anyone else, but for him it's now as natural as breathing—check your perimeter, always know everything around you.

He sits at Ms. Jenkins' desk. As he sits, he realizes and thinks to himself, *Damn, I've got my back to the door.*

Diego feels the need to turn around, to cover his six. But this Jenkins chick can't see him lose it. *Don't act crazy right now, Sanchez.* He needs to calm his nerves, but the moments are turning into hours. He feels himself sweating, but is he really sweating or is it nerves? The next logical thought is, *Does she have any idea what is going on in my head?* He stares maybe a bit too hard at her to gauge where she is.

His left foot is moving up and down, his knee is bouncing a bit. Can she it? Diego hates that he can't be the person he was before his time overseas. He feels the sweat now going coldly down his neck and onto his back—it itches. He does a hard blink to refocus and get his bearings. He moves his gaze to her desk. She's in a bad place with him there. Does she know that he could kill her with about six or seven of the things within his reach on her desk? How could she not know that? It makes him angry; he feels the flush cover his face, and his ears are even hot.

Calm down, Diego, he cooly thinks to himself.

"Mr. Sanchez, what skills do you have?" Ms. Jenkins says.

He can't hide that the question annoys him. What is he supposed to do or say?

He wants to stand up and scream in her face, *Bitch, I'm a fucking soldier! There is nothing I can't do. I work on and repair my weapons, vehicles, and all my equipment! I'm an...* It hurts his heart when he has to change his thought. "I was an NCO. I took care of my soldiers— they're my family. I was trained to do what is necessary."

A sad and lonely man, he continues to rail on in his mind. *There is nothing I'm not qualified to do! You sit here at this desk—you fucking judge me? I was... You know what, I* am *and always will be a soldier.* His mind is moving a million miles an hour, but outside he is quietly sitting there like he is deep in thought. If he speaks out loud, they'll take him out of here screaming.

They call me a baby killer, a murderer, and they say that following orders is no excuse for what I did. It wasn't just following orders, cunt!

His breathing is picking up. How long has he

sat here without saying a word to her? He needs to say something, but nothing civil comes to mind. He needs to bring it down a notch; he needs to get back in control. But his mind rages ahead.

It was my duty! It was my life! And you sit here and judge me? How dare you? His hands are fidgeting, and he can feel his eyes darting. *How about you just sit there and say thank you. Because of me and my friends, you have the right to...burn flags, carry guns, and plead the fifth to save your ass. You can say what you want about our government and our country, travel where you want and just live FREELY! Because of me and my soldiers. My brothers who died to give you slimy, worthless pieces of garbage the freedoms that you spit on! Yes, there is nothing that I cannot accomplish, because the Army taught me to be a survivor.*

His mind just took over for… How long? He comes back; Ms. Jenkins is waiting for his answer. Diego makes eye contact for the first time in moments and she sits tapping her pen in a, *"Hurry up, will ya'."* motion. How long has she waited?

"Mr. Sanchez, is everything okay?" she says with a bit of an edge. *I must have been gone for a while.*

With a small breath, "Yes, ma'am. I'm okay. Umm, yes, uhh… My job was in artillery. But I have been trained in vehicle repair and maintenance, I have driven two-ton vehicles and Humvees over large distances. I was a platoon sergeant; I was in charge of four squads of men. I trained and ensured that my soldiers were in good physical and mental condition for our missions.”

As impressive as it all sounded to him, he sees a judgy stupid look from her. Ms. Jenkins gives a woeful but polite smile. “Mr. Sanchez, I am sure that some of those skills are transferable to what we can prepare for you. Do you have any work experience outside of the military?”

Diego thinks to himself for a moment; he was surprised by the question. Why would she ask that? He had been in charge of men and multi-million-dollar equipment. He had traveled the world representing his country. So why ask that? With a confused glance, he opens his mouth.

“No, ma’am. After my high school graduation, within a month I had gone to boot camp. My work history is my last 15 years in the Army.”

“That’s just fine,” she says and gives that

same sad smile. "You have *some* transferable skills. We'll find something for you. I'm confident of that."

She has lost him. *Some transferrable skills? Really?* What the fuck just happened? Yeah, this conversation is over.

Diego is now completely over this interview. His mind is again evaluating the room. He can't calm down. It irritates him to be sitting in front of this woman—*A kid, because of a fucking college diploma, gets to judge me? What has she ever done besides going down on a few frat guys on a weekend?* He feels his anger welling up.

His eyes are darting about. He's having a mind wreck right about now. *A mind wreck?*

He giggles to himself. He hadn't thought of

that phrase since the last deployment. What does it mean?

A mind wreck is the moment you realize that the moment has become a clusterfuck. A moment or time that is beyond repair… Others call it FUBAR. Not Sgt. Sanchez: that nugget he had passed on to his soldiers.

Ms. Jenkins types, looks at her computer screen, and continues to ask questions. He can only stare at her manicured nails. That nail job probably costs a huge amount of money. And she only went to college. She has never served her country. Never has she risked her life for anyone!

Diego, for his part, absent-mindedly continues to answer her bullshit questions. What is she going to find for a career soldier? A man that spent his adult life learning to blow things up from miles away. A man that has killed…killed man, woman, and (sadly) child. It isn't an easy night's sleep without his meds.

Why am I even here? Oh yeah, my head wasn't right enough to be a soldier any longer. When you're satisfied with, and don't mind, being a killer, even other soldiers begin to judge you. He continues to stare blankly and he's back in the desert. Yes, that day… The last day. "Sgt. Sanchez, they're dead." That brought him back from the deep.

Diego will say he doesn't remember much about that last hour. Maybe he just wants to forget that last hour that he was still a platoon sergeant. Yeah, maybe these last few kills were not "necessary." But he had not been able to stop. With no mercy. No, he had not shown any mercy… He walked into an area where there had been sniper fire within the last few hours. His first squad had wasted that piece of trash.

They took over the village in short order, his men had been going about it in the most business-like manner possible. That was when all hell broke loose.

The next thing he saw was the look on everyone's faces. *Fuck them*—that was Diego's first clear thought—the next he knew, he heard those fateful words…

"Sgt. Sanchez, they're dead." The voice of his soldier and the hand on his shoulder brought him back. Back from where? That's a very tough question.

A soldier can't tell you where that place is. Where a soldier goes when they kill. A place where—now this will blow your mind—a place where you will never ever leave. Where you kill. Where there is nothing but hate and rage on the outside, but this sickening feeling of calm and control deep inside. Where you go to stay away from feeling any guilt. Where you do the killing, till the Killing Man comes…

But what you don't know, don't see, or just don't want to say… You are the Killing Man. Diego had had enough of these people. The mission was to save these people. The soldiers were there to help these sorry, shitty people. They protect the bombers, the snipers, and the locals that are our enemies. Yes, they protected this sniper fuck that took two of SFC Sanchez's soldiers.

That was it. That exact event. He had never admitted this, even as he was being medically discharged back at home, it was the deaths of his soldiers. And these fucking people did nothing. So, after snapping, Diego lined up all the people from the village his platoon had entered.

The statements from all the soldiers on site said that Diego started with the children. He drew his side arm, he told the people why he was doing what he did; he was more machine at this time than person. He had instructed the soldiers to keep the adults back. All it took was one bullet to each of their tiny foreheads.

The statements about this part were things of pure horror. The other soldiers feared for their lives if they did not listen to the demands from their leader.

Learning this made him queasy. How many children were in that line? Ten, maybe? Twelve? A single bullet as their parents, grandparents, and siblings (who were next) looked on at the carnage. That is what his soldiers had called what he had done: "pure carnage." The statements said that even his soldiers had become sick, why had he not seen that? Diego wondered, "*Did I point my weapon at them when they moved toward me? I don't remember.*"

"*Christ, I really don't remember.*"

The doctors that had interviewed him asked him over and over. And Diego stated over and over that he had left his thoughts. The last thing he remembered was seeing his soldiers after first squad had taken out the sniper. Then it was the hand on his shoulder and the statement of the villagers being dead.

SPC John Davis, Official Statement:

"SFC Sanchez just snapped when he saw Winters and Jones on the ground. When he instructed us to begin lining up the villagers, we thought he was attempting to root out other insurgents. We figured he was just going to smoke them out by yelling at their children. God knows I never would have gathered children to watch him execute them. I've killed in my time, but to survive. He left his senses. There is no way a sane man does what SFC Sanchez did. His laugh—that laugh in the middle of everything. It was horrible. He was a good man, I don't know what happened to him."

END of Official Statement.

"You made me do this," Diego yelled as he took

his time, savored the moments… "You protect your killers, they killed my soldiers. Each soldier in my platoon is my child, my responsibility to bring home! So you will watch me take your children, each one of them!"

Diego continued to walk down the line. Was it seven or eight? Who cares, they're all dying today. He let out a single sickening laugh. It was more like a cackle. And he continued till he emptied, reloaded, and emptied every magazine he had on hand.

The platoon, with their weapons at their sides and staring in disbelief, looked at one another. SFC Sanchez had lost it. But if they tried to stop him, it could be dangerous for them. Hell, he'd been waving his weapon at the soldiers that had moved forward to stop the families. As he finished with the children, he threw down the side arm and grabbed one of the M-16s left by the soldiers killed by the sniper.

SGT Richard Steiner, Official Statement:

"SFC Sanchez is one of the best men I ever had the pleasure of having as a leader and mentor. What happened on that day is truly reprehensible and there is no excuse. As a squad leader, I could understand how upset he was as we found our guys dead from sniper fire. We had been assisting this village for a few days. Liberating them. Then they hide that sniper. He was not a human after that. After laughing while shooting the children and emptying his side arm, he reached down and

grabbed one of our buddies' M-16s. He calmly beganfiring. He mumbled something about, 'Sanchez, one shot one kill.' He never missed. They tried running, but he was so accurate. Every shot was to kill. We couldn't save any of them; had we stepped in, he would have shot us as well. At least that was my assessment. I told my squad to scramble. I believe the other squad leaders did the same."

END of Official Statement.

Yep, Diego had had a mind wreck. The others could only stare as he opened fire. It was quick and efficient. SFC Sanchez, if nothing else, was a crack shot. He leveled the weapon and opened fire. Man or woman, he didn't care; he killed the ones that began to run first. The others who froze or raised their hands in surrender died with the foolish thought that they would be spared for raising their hands.

Diego Sanchez, class of 1995. Most likely to be forgotten… An afterthought to everyone in his class. All he'd ever wanted was to be a soldier. To have the respect that soldiers got. To be thanked for his service, to protect his country, to die if need be. He stayed in shape on his own, running and lifting weights, learning about the military. It would be his career. He would never come back here, fuck all these high school kids. After graduation, he knew that he would never want to nor have to speak to any of these people again. Throughout his school days, he did enough to stay invisible. No clubs, sports, or competitions—it was all preparation for his military life.

Now, 15 years on, he would forever be remembered by the men of his platoon for a hateful and callous act. He shifted from trusted and heralded leader to merciless killer in the span of seven or eight minutes. He had ended his career.

The clarity came to him after he had emptied the last magazine at his disposal. When he didn't have a magazine immediately handy, a soldier finally stepped in. Diego then heard the first clear words he could remember in, what, seven or eight minutes? "Sgt. Sanchez, they're dead." The soldier sounded somber; he spoke quietly and sounded like he was just a bit in shock. Diego turned (the official statements claimed) and he was still smiling when he looked at them.

Then it was over. Just as it had started, it was

over. Really, everything was over. He was not aware yet, but his career would last the few months it took for him to be arrested, evaluated, and chaptered medically from the Army.

He laid the weapon at his feet; the smile began to wane. He sort of crumpled to the ground, actually taking a knee, staring at it for a moment. Then he looked at the stack of bodies which he had laid to waste. He laughed one last time (a pitiful and tired breath, really) and spoke clearly for the first time since the incident started, staring at the tower where first platoon had laid waste to the sniper: "Fucking snipers, they're real pieces of shit."

He took a deep breath and wiped his face and eyes with the heels of his hands. Maybe it was tears, some of the men thought, but most thought correctly that his manic state had made him sweaty and tired. The moments ticked slowly; the world was moving in slow-motion. He looked off into the distance. He was nowhere at the moment. He took a moment to look at his work. *It would have been impressive*, he thought, *if it hadn't been a massacre.* Again, he rubbed his eyes and stared at all the dead villagers. Victims. Yeah, Diego clearly thought that they would all be considered his victims.

"*Fuck 'em!*" It was his first clear thought in seven or eight minutes.

By this time, other platoons and platoon leaders had made their way to what sounded like a major fire-fight, only to see SFC Sanchez removing a wrinkled pack of cigarettes from his left breast pocket, pulling out one cigarette, and then lighting it, still observing his work. Some soldier statements claimed that he began laughing again at what lay before him. Taking deep drags of his cigarette, trying to get that light head rush that only the really deep drags give you. It was a sickening, raspy laugh to those that heard it.

Diego wasn't sure who did it; the next few minutes were just as confusing as the mind wreck was to him. He was told to stand, so he took a last drag from his cigarette and stood up. Instinctively he raised his hands. No one tells you to stand up after a wicked mind wreck without them having a weapon on you (and there were a few that he could see) and heavy trigger fingers. He looked square into the L-T's face, cracked a weary smile, and just said, "Let's go, sir."

He self-reported the incident. He took full and sole responsibility for what had happened. The medical board determined that he'd had a break in reality. That he was "sick." So the Army medically boarded him within a few months. The incident was kept quiet, which was not difficult. Every villager, every single one, had been killed. No witnesses or people to pay compensation for their losses. As shitty as it might sound to civilians, it could have been a real black eye for the Army. As it stood, the entire thing disappeared from the face of the earth. Diego understood, business decisions like that were made every day.

The Army, his family. His life's work. His brothers. They didn't want him anymore. It was that fact that hurt the most. Everything that he had done for his country over the last fifteen years. His sacrifices, his field time, contacting families of dead soldiers, killing in the name of freedom and the United States. All that, and he would be thrown out like yesterday's garbage? Never to be a soldier again. That was all he had ever wanted, and now it was gone. No more respect. That would be the hardest part.

Luckily for him, even with what he had done, the doctors in-service (and the VA evaluators) determined he wasn't a danger to the public. So, yes, like yesterday's leftovers, he was thrown out.

Diego thought of it as being thrown away. After fifteen years of his life, his entire adult life, he would now be a civilian. The strange thing is…he doesn't know how to be a civilian.

That reality scared him more than any night

fire missions or ammo dumps. The Army was his wife and children. They left him. At 33 years old…he was alone. Truly alone. He would never go back to his hometown; it was backwoods, a hick piece of garbage in the middle of nowhere. Besides, his family quit giving a shit about him years ago. The only person he had ever cared for was his grandfather anyway.

His grandfather had been a soldier and carried himself in that manner till the day he died. His grandfather had shown him that being a soldier was the best way of life. His parents only reached out when they needed money. Diego had no brothers or sisters; his parents were lazy. His mother had stopped working to raise him (what a joke that was) and his father was a leech that worked for anyone that would pay him under the table. Now that they were older, he could no longer work the types of jobs that could pay him what he needed. Because neither of them had any real earnings or money, there would be no Social Security. So, they got welfare. And still, they couldn't make ends meet. They would occasionally reach out to ask for money. Never about how he was doing or if was he safe. It had been years since he'd actually answered or returned any of their calls, yet they didn't get the hint. He had no use for them.

So, for the first time in his adult life, he was not a soldier. And the first thing he knew was that he was not going "home." He had never wanted to return there. His home was the Army. And not only would he never return to the little town where he started life, but he would never be able to return to the family and home. So, alone, he moves—far enough from post that he will never see a soldier that might know him, but close enough so that he can go to the VA.

In the distance, he hears a voice. *Where am I?* was his first thought. The second: *How long was I gone? Did I stop answering her questions?*

"Mr. Sanchez? Are you listening to me?" It was Ms. Jenkins. Again it crosses his mind: how long had he been gone?

"I'm sorry, ma'am, you have my undivided attention." Finally, he was clear and back.

"Mr. Sanchez, right now there are no jobs available for you." The sorority girl's voice came out of her. The business voice, the one Diego thought she practiced, had dropped. She was done.

"What?" he says, furrowing his brows, very

perplexed. "Nothing? I led platoons, I—"

She abruptly raises a hand to stop him. "I'm really sorry, I know that you want to work, but I can't really send you out to look for jobs without warning the employers of—"

"Wait! Wait just a goddamn minute! What do you mean warning? There is no fucking warning to give to anyone!" He can feel his face getting flushed with anger. The blood has worked its way to his face and ears. When he began to get really angry, it was like that old wife's tale about someone talking about you: his ears began to burn.

Diego finally thinks to himself, *"Calm down, fucko! You're scaring her."*

Knowing that she likely had a panic button or safety word or action, Diego speaks again, this time in a calm manner. "Look, ma'am, I need to work. My disability is just enough to get by. I lost any chance of a pension with my medical discharge. Please…please, I'll do anything."

Ms. Jenkins, trying to remain calm, begins to speak, but Diego notices that her right hand has disappeared. *Five bucks says she does have a panic button. In a few seconds, an office manager or supervisor will show up and stand to the side. It's the guard from the front of the office, he'll try to walk up behind me.*

That guard will attempt to surprise me. That thought makes Diego laugh to himself. He'd sized that guy up when he walked in. He's a non-threat, even with a gun. Physically, he's sloppy and even looks quite slow. He has a weapon on his left hip—

a southpaw. If he knew anything at all, he'd bring his right foot forward. That way, Diego thought, he could keep his weapon as far away from Diego as possible.

Like clockwork, the supervisor appears behind Ms. Jenkins, but at least he's trying to act nonchalant—he's at the printer. Looking through a stack of papers, waiting for the security guard to appear… Like magic, Diego hears him walking up behind him, maybe 15 to 20 feet away. He drags his feet and walks quite loudly.

He blankly stares at Ms. Jenkins. Why did she do that? He could have reeled everything back into a controlled point. Now there would be trouble. It could have been avoided. *Fucking Ms. Jenkins*, he thought.

Diego is completely aware. He's ready for war—a war they did not want, but that they had started. *If the southpaw touches me*, thought Diego, *I'll break his hand.* Diego begins moving his thumbs across the tips of his fingers. It's a habit that he'd started while still in the Army when he would go to hot zones: rubbing his thumbs against each fingertip woke up his senses. It prepared his mind to fight.

Diego thinks to himself, *The guard needs to just stand there. Yeah, that would be the best thing for everyone here.* Three to four feet now, Diego is on full alert; he scans Ms. Jenkins' desk for the weapons he'd identified earlier, should he need one. Lucky for the guy, Diego begins to breathe slowly and will control his urges today.

Diego simply states in a voice just loud enough for the supervisor and the guard to hear, "I see that we're done here, right?"

"I'm afraid so, Mr. Sanchez," Ms. Jenkins says in a relieved tone. Diego stands, staring at her as he does. He cannot hide his anger. Although he is controlling his breathing, he's clearly bothered. And he stares just long enough to scare her. Since she contacted the guard and supervisor, creeping her out is the least he can do.

As Diego turns, she quietly breathes a sigh of relief. The supervisor walks over and puts a hand on her shoulder to calm her. *The crazy man is leaving,* she thinks to herself. All those years of college to put up with people like this. She wants to leave right now. She can't do this. Why did she ever want to be a social worker? Ms. Jenkins slowly lays her face in her hands and begins to quietly weep. She keeps thinking of his eyes, wide and glaring. How quickly he had changed; it was like a light switch. The look was pure evil. In her short life she'd never witnessed true evil. Ms. Jenkins knows that she has just seen the Devil. And she knows that she never wants to see him again.

Diego reads into her eyes as he turns. With a quiet laugh, he thinks to himself, *you were too scared of me to do this job, Ms. Jenkins. But pushing that button might have been the smartest thing you did today. Still, though, fuck you, lady.* He quietly continues to walk away, the supervisor and guard both stand there like they did something. The supervisor looks like he's trying to get laid by the now-spooked Ms. Jenkins, and the guard looks like he'll have a story for his grandkids: The day he scared a crazy guy out of the office. Little does that man know, Diego could have killed him ten times over. And enjoyed it.

The only thing they did was piss me off. Diego shoots a look back at each of them as he continues to leave. He can't stop thinking that the shitty guard will remember this moment forever; yeah, he made a veteran leave the office. He'll jerk off to that memory tonight… Another laugh as he continues his walk out of the office.

Diego is fed up at the moment; he feels the fresh air on his face, but he knows his face is flush from the anger still in his belly. He walks toward his vehicle. He needs to go to the grocery store; he has no food at home. Why would he think of food?

"Fuck me." He breathes the words out and sits down in the driver's seat of his car. He leaves the government building behind: Ms. Jenkins, the horny supervisor, and Diego's favorite, the southpaw guard. They're quickly becoming a distant memory. He floats toward his local grocery store to buy some dinner and a sixer. As usual, he takes a different route. *Never get complacent, change your route every time!* Since coming home from his first deployment, he's always felt that any vehicle behind him for more than two blocks might be a threat. It was a gift that war had given him.

He aimlessly wanders around the store; he has his beer and a rotisserie chicken. He doesn't need or want anything else—he honestly doesn't want to go home. The loneliness is grating on him. He comes closer every single day to walking off a building. After the military let him go, he had to agree to never have in his possession or available to him any weapons: firearms. God, what he would do to have one gun, one bullet; just one chance to eat that bullet and rest.

The nights and the little sleep his mind allow him are troublesome on the best nights. It sucks. He should have eaten a bullet and chased his "victims" into the afterlife. Goddammit, why couldn't he have saved one bullet? Had he been in any sort of control, he would have done just that.

"One shot, one kill. That would be great," he says under his breath as he's checking out. He grabs his receipt and walks toward the front doors, still feeling unsure about heading home, being alive, or hurting someone. He finds that the thoughts of violence give him peace. Violence is more welcome in his mind than the looks from the doctors, social workers, and government officials that still judge him and his every action when he's in their presence.

He steps into the crosswalk. Diego doesn't look either way; there are stop signs on each side. His concentration is broken by a honk…

"The fuck…" Diego immediately shoots a look at the driver. The man, a fake tough guy (Diego sees it in his eyes), honks again. This is what Diego needs. This man will likely think that he wants to engage him. There's a woman next to him, so he'll want to look tough for her, but the thing Diego really likes is that the driver has two buddies in the truck's second row that will definitely push him.

"We got a problem?" the driver says out his open window. Diego hears Tweedle-Dee and Tweedle-Dum laugh. *Yes, this is going to get fun real quick.*

With a smile that no one ever wanted to see on Diego's face again, he opens his mouth to speak. "I don't have a problem…" He drops the beer and chicken to the ground. He begins to slowly walk toward the car. "But you, you have a problem now."

Calmly he continues to move toward the car. He sees the driver's eyes widen in fear. The driver looks over his shoulder at his buddies in the backseat. The driver's girl looks toward the very calm Diego and says something to her boyfriend. She's the smartest person in that vehicle; she knows to be worried about this guy walking toward them. He has almost made it to the driver's door and is stepping past the driver's side fender.

I hope he has a gun, Diego thinks briefly. Just then, he stops. He gives a thoughtful look at the vehicle. What crosses his mind is that he doesn't want to get ambushed by the two in the back. Diego has a thought. "Why don't we talk about your problem out here?" He raises his hand and does a little Bruce Lee "come and get some" signal to the driver. "Step out here and we'll talk."

All the time, the former soldier is watching the back seat—the hands of the men are on the front seat. That's a good sign; if they had guns, they would be pointed at him by now. No, this man is going to step out all alone. Fear and over-confidence are a terrible mix. They force you into poor decisions.

The driver opens the door. He blusters and blows wind about Diego not knowing who he's messing with, how Diego should turn his old ass around, he and his homies are going to blah, blah, blah.

Diego's smile widens; he's cutting the distance between the two of them. He has assessed the entirety of the current situation, and here's the lay of the land.

What the man doesn't know is:

1. Diego sees the gun in his waistband.

2. Diego is now close enough to the man that the driver is in more danger than he would care to know.

3. One of them is not leaving this parking lot alive.

"So what you wanna' do, man?" Still blustering.

Diego, still moving slowly toward the man, speaks once again. "I want you to take that gun out. I want you to please, please take that gun out!" The second time he says it, he finally sounds angry. And the man, foolishly, stands still.

"You're crazy, man. Pick up your beer and get the fuck out—"

Diego moves swiftly, with malice in mind, toward the man. Quickly, he kicks the door shut and snatches the man by his t-shirt. Diego easily throws him upon the hood and begins to wail on his face.

"Thank you, fucker! I've been waiting for you," Diego yells as he continues to pound the man's face. There comes that laugh: it's the creepiest thing—at least that's what his soldiers said. Out of the corner of his eye, he sees the driver's side door begin to open. Diego continues his assault on the guy; he's baiting the man opening the door. If he waits just long enough…

The man's head and shoulder pop out. He's saying something, but not for long. Diego looks over and smiles that smile, which puts the man at a pause just long enough for Diego to pick up his right leg and crush the man in the door with a swift kick. Somewhere in the distance, he hears the smart girlfriend screaming for help. Diego glances for friend number two—he's a smart cookie as well, he's stayed glued to his seat.

Diego is done pummeling the man. The man lies upon his hood and is a bloody mess. He's crying and he's pissed himself. Diego thinks about how often he's seen men cry and piss themselves when in danger. Not just danger though. Death. He continues to laugh and removes the gun from the man's waistband.

The pistol grip feels like home. It's like a government-issued 9mm handgun. By the weight, Deigo knows it's a standard 17-round clip. The weapon is light in his hand and his mind is ready to get back to work. For the first time since the incident began, he notices the many people watching the event. At least they know enough to stay away.

"You should have laid off the horn, piss-pants. You fucked the pooch on that one." Grabbing the weeping man by his shirt, Diego throws him to the ground and stands over him, still laughing a bit. He steps a few feet away; he feels in full command with the weapon in his hand. He grips it tightly, the unfortunate owner of the gun still weeping. Diego does a military about-face and stares at the beaten man.

"You could be somewhere else. You could be heading home. Maybe getting your pecker wet tonight with the chick in the truck. Instead, you're going to be part of a murder scene. All because you fucked around to look tough." Diego squats and taps the man on the forehead with his own gun. "You're a young guy, you should have known that when you fuck around, eventually you will find out. And today is that day for you."

Diego removes the clip and begins to slowly

empty it, dropping bullet after bullet on the bloody man's chest, making sure there is one bullet remaining. That's all he needs.

Blubbering at the words he's just heard, the man begs for his life. "Please, please don't kill me…"

Diego stares intently. He quickly slams the clip with and single round into the gun and chambers that round. He leans in and chooses his next words carefully. "Kill you? There's more life left for you. I meant…me."

Diego quickly turns the gun toward himself, puts the barrel in his mouth, aims up toward his brain, and shuts his lights out. There are screams all over the parking lot. The weeping man screams as he is covered with Diego's skull, brain matter, and feces. The woman in the front seat has seen everything and will spend years in therapy remembering the man's actions. The friend that did nothing lays his face into his hands and cannot believe what has transpired. Still on the ground and bleeding, the other man lies quietly and stares on in shock.

But Diego had finally turned out the lights.

As he prepared to finish his journey, Diego had some clear thoughts. Again, he numbered them carefully.

1. He knew everything that had happened back in that village. The truth of the matter was that he did snap, but it was more like he was just fed up. He'd had his fill of his soldiers being killed. So fuck it. As he was firing on those people, he came up with the next

steps. He'd have to convince the doctors, the social workers, and himself that he blacked out. His miscalculation was getting medically discharged. He thought maybe it'd be some hospital time and then he'd go back to work. Well, he screwed the pooch on that one. As he was ending everything, he figured that he could at least admit that to himself.

2. Beating that man was just for fun. The real gamble had been hoping that he had a weapon on him. Diego couldn't be sure until he had the man out of the vehicle. The man was never going to die, but he will think twice before he ever threatens anyone again.

3. The man really did fuck around and find out what happens when you underestimate the situation.

4. Finally, and this made him smile as his finger pulled the trigger: This was the only time that he'd hear the

bullet that ended him. The irony of that made a small laugh; the last sound that the man consciously made.

The former soldier, murderer, and man lies on the ground, blood spilling from his mouth, and his aim has left a big exit wound in the rear side of his head.

People had been recording, streaming, and photographing the entire thing. The man's body looks a bit gray as he expires. People that had only seen dead bodies on television and movies were in for a treat. They say that the smell of death is something you never forget. But the soldier knows that the smell is shit. Yep, when people die, their bowels release—that's just a tidbit for the kiddies.

The violent end of the man, the disgraced

soldier, reverberates through the veteran community. There should have been help for him. Why was he walking the streets? This dangerous, skilled killer walked amongst regular people. The newspapers are filled with the story of the soldier that committed suicide in a parking lot.

In death, Diego has done more to bring light to the plight of soldiers that are back from war. The reality is that the saddest part of becoming a great soldier is that you perfect a few skills. You can work without sleep, and you find a way to function regardless of the surroundings. You can look another human in the face, and in the next moment you can end their life. The saddest moment for families is when they get someone back that is not who they sent away. They get a voided life.

Some soldiers die and, for that reason, never really come back home. The unfortunate ones return home, but never come home. After war, there is no home. Soldiers return as shells of humans. They are what they were trained to be, what the fighting, killing, and surviving made them. Soldiers.

Solitude:

The Insomniac's Lullaby

Part 1:

"It's 4 o'clock in the morning, Dammit listen to me good..."

Sir Elton John, "Someone Saved My Life Tonight"

Yet another night of sleep eludes his anxious mind. Why? Good question, but is it the right one? How long has it been since he's slept? Days, maybe weeks… Every time he walks past a mirror, he notices that he appears to be getting more pale, the bags under his eyes growing darker by the day. After "admiring" himself in the mirror, he finds himself staring out the dingy windows that allow in what little natural light can fight its way into the old apartment. Below are the sounds of the ongoing vicious world that many still call dog-eat-dog. He wonders if leaping from the fourth floor would just leave him lying in a pile of alive, broken, pain-riddled angst? Failing at committing suicide brings a wry smile to his unshaved, pale face.

"Goddamn, but ain't that a fucked up thing! Jumping from any height trying to end your life, but you're too stupid to get it right." As the thought settles in his mind, the smile quickly fades away, and his mind moves to a very clear and sobering thought.

"*Still* alive? You aren't alive right now, are you?" Talking to himself has become his main source of entertainment and solace. "Just my luck, I fall on a fat woman walking by. I end her life and her girth saves mine." Sure, 40 feet would really hurt, but not quite the ending he wants.

The insomniac was not always this angry,

rail-thin, confused man. He had been a bit heavier (never overweight), quiet and reserved, and he used to keep his dark hair, nails, and body in a clean and neat state. That changed when the sleep stopped. Now he was floating most days, and most of the things he sees aren't real anymore. It was a bit scary at first, but he's gotten used to the hallucinations. Hell, he kind of likes them to keep him company in the middle of the night.

He leans back against a wall and reaches for a soda can that's halfway empty. He has to get his head right, and being right is thinking of and creating scenarios of living with the darkness that engulfs his mind and time.

To start, he steps out of the flood of streetlights, horns, and people yelling that fills his apartment's living room, slyly walking into the bathroom. It's something that he had started doing lately. When the sun began to settle each evening, he would walk into the darker recesses of his apartment. Many people cannot, or will not, recognize that there are things in the dark.

Things being the operative word. Things that defy the descriptions of the rested eye. Why though? It's simple, he thought as each search began. Rested eyes see too clearly to be fooled by the things in the darkness. Rested eyes are the actual windows to the soul. Tired eyes, his eyes specifically, are susceptible to being fooled by the darkness. He would tell himself that once he rested, the things in the dark would disappear. He just needed to sleep first.

He delves ever deeper into the darkened apartment, all the while looking for the fearsome things that do not exist in the eyes of others, but he remembers one extremely important fact that you must never forget in the dark: Once those things do catch up to you, once you are face to face with them, you can't get away. So far, though, he had not been caught. A few words to the wise—he has started using "word to the wise" as a blanket statement for survival in this insomniac life— stay close to the walls, *dick tight*, as you enter the room. Know the location of all light switches. And always turn the light source on before entering and lowering your guard. As he glanced into his smelly green bathroom and saw the other parts of nightmare things, it made him think of the power of mirrors. Mirrors and the dark; Christ, that's a scary combination.

"Don't get me started," he mumbles as makes his way out of his pajamas and into a nice hot shower. Each day that he spends in his small apartment, he notices he has less and less a need, or even a want, to leave his sanctuary. Inside this space, he is king. He wears whatever he likes, eats wherever and whatever he pleases! But why does he love to be alone?

Alone, no one is there to stab you in the back, make fun of you and your life, or spread their lies and theories about why you are such a failure. His theories don't need challenges—for example, he believes in the truth of mirrors and their power.

Mirrors—and this is just his honest belief—can hold onto images and the energy of someone that stares into them. How does he know this little tidbit? Every dirty apartment or foster home he's ever stayed in had a host of mirrors that held the pain, negative energy, and sadness of previous residents. Those mirrors literally darken the rooms where they hang. But you'll never see it if you aren't looking. It's like a simple person being hypnotized or possessed. You must be prepared to accept what the world is showing you. You'll waste a lifetime pretending not to have seen what you have just seen. Why? Because no one is prepared to hear about the things that go bump in the night.

Another fact is that the dark is violent and scary. And no, the insomnia didn't start this belief. He's known this since he was a child. The dark, as you should also know, is a different world. There are different rules. What starts in the dark will hide in the day.

Meaning that all of those midnight rendezvous and night missions might not be seen by everyone, but they are seen by those brave enough to stare into that darkness and wait for what it has to show them.

You can't stop the darkness once it starts. Once it starts… Ahh, yes, the darkness can make you feel confident.

"Nobody sees me. I'm innocent in the dark." He has said that so many times, but it sees—yes, the world sees everything. Your thoughts should always remind you that there are video doorbells, cameras hanging on every intersection and corner, and insomniacs staring into the void at all hours.

He feels utter sadness at the contempt that he holds for this truly fucked up and rancid world. He grabs a fresh match, lights it, and then sets fire to his Zig-Zag-wrapped goodie.

He allows himself a moment to reflect on a life that he lived long ago…

It's 1978, and a young boy sits atop a three-step cement porch. The house is government funded; his surroundings are never clean and never quiet. It's Christmas break, chilly but never really cold here in East Texas. He woke up early, Christmas is tomorrow, and his dad said that he would be here today. He sincerely hates his mother for chasing his father away. The boy only trusts his dad—*Dad hasn't, wouldn't, and doesn't lie to me. Dad always shows up when I need him.* The young boy, thin and tall for his age, headed out very early. He wants to be the first person to lays eyes on his dad…

The boy has been outside all day, and his mother brings lunch to him. He needs to use the bathroom, but he's sure that the moment he leaves, Dad will pull right up into the driveway. And if Dad pulls up and the boy isn't there, then Dad won't know how much that he's wanted here.

I want Dad here! the boy thinks to himself as he hears his sister and brother, the twins, watching TV. *Maybe they don't want Dad here, but I do.* The boy is the oldest of the three kids. He remembers dad better than anyone else.

The sun has started to pull its blankets up to its chin. It may be East Texas, but as the sun is setting, the temperature is dropping quickly.

It has gotten late. The boy hasn't seen or sensed his mother periodically checking on him. She silently cries as she hears the boy take a deep breath every time a car approaches, then quickly exhales as each car passes by.

His mother, a drab and plain lady in her late 20s, loves her children and would never speak ill of their father. Especially to her oldest son, as he remembers his father better than the younger children. The boy will never know what Mom went through with "that man." Drinking beer after beer and whiskey shots between each was enough to make the boy's mother want to escape. But where would she go?

The things that children will never know;

those are the things that eat at their parents.

The parents had met while Mom was still in high school. The father had dropped out, but younger women always go for the bad boy. So, the boy came along within a year of their first meeting. She would leave school to support herself and her budding family.

In the first year or so, life had been good. But the father was not just a bad boy in looks and attitude. He had his own business, and the weed business in the 70s was good. But along with that came alcohol, and he liked to indulge in cocaine. When they had gotten together, the man was solidly built with a flowing mane of dark hair, his blue eyes set off perfectly against his tan skin. She felt lucky to be with him;

together they made a gorgeous couple. And their first child had been the cherry on top. Then he started getting very high off his own supply, so the money problems started. And the monkey on his back wanted more and more. As Guns N' Roses would sing in the 80s, "He used to do a little, but a little wouldn't do it, so the little got more and more." In the beginning, he thought it would all fall into place. That never happened.

The nightly beatings and sex that may as well have been rape had started after one of the first times he came up short to his suppliers.

At first, they beat him and broke bones. So, of course, he took it out on her. Then, when they grew weary of hurting him, they showed up at the dinky apartment where he lived with his girl and their baby.

On this occasion, he thought they would hurt the girl or the kid. He begged them off, but they told him they had other plans. In walked Jam—a business associate and the main muscle for the biggest supplier in the area—and two large Mexican men in old t-shirts and jeans. The larger of the two had long stringy hair that flowed past his shoulders, and his strapless t-shirt showed muscle upon muscle rippling underneath, with tattoos up and down his arms and on his chest. He looked cocky and angry, ready to snap as he peered about the shack where the family lived. The second man was even larger, but not muscular.

He was probably just bull strong. This man had a stench about him, like he had been slaughtering cattle or pigs for days and had not bathed. The smell was disgusting and somehow intimidating at the same time.

The final visitor was the enforcer's boss. The man knew instantly that this was the man in charge; though he had never met him, this man walked differently. He walked in and you knew he feared nothing and no one. The boss was calm, quiet, and elegant. He wore a custom grey suit with a light blue shirt and red tie, wing-tipped black shoes, and his hair was short and well combed. If the insomniac could remember this man, he'd know where his ideas of the dark had come from, as this man was engulfed in darkness—a snake that no one should ever bother. He walked about the apartment staring down his nose at surroundings he considered far below him. The snake slithered toward the woman, who clutched her boy as tight as possible, but it didn't help. He deftly took the child from his mother, all the while staring straight at her, almost daring her to say a word. He nuzzled the child like he cared, but this man cared about nothing and no one.

He told her that no harm would come to the child, he simply wanted to hand the boy to his father. He did exactly as he said: he walked over to his wayward employee and sat next to him. He looked at him and quietly said, "Take your boy now."

The man slowly took the child and took a deep breath. He was utterly confused as to what the end game would be now.

What happened next would go on for maybe thirty minutes. In the man's mind, it lasted forever. He would clutch his child closely, tightly, and his tears would fall on the child's blanket wrap.

The two large men walked over to the woman. They roughly picked her up and stood on either side of her. They then began tearing her clothes off and grabbing at her naked body. The heavyset man threw her on the couch and grabbed her by the hair with a hammy left hand; with his right hand, he began to unbutton his jeans.

She looked to her man; he, in return, tried to look down at his child. The boss, now leaning back, smoking a cigar, and getting ready to enjoy a show, cleared his throat and told him to enjoy the show, and if he looked away again, he would ensure that things would get much worse for her than initially intended. The man knew this was not a warning, but a promise. His heart sank as he looked at his woman with another man's dick shoved in her mouth.

The other muscular man, now undressed, grabbed the woman by her hips and thrust himself inside her. They turned her over, flipped her around, and shared her until they both finished, one inside her and one on her face. They laughed, high-fived, and got dressed, speaking to each other in Spanish. They looked over at their boss, who gave them a *job well done* look.

So, the man held his child, wept, and watched the two large men zip up and leave. The muscled-up man even winked at the weeping man on his way out of the apartment. It had gone on for a long time; they would tell her what to do and remind her to look at her man while she did their bidding. She cried the entire time. Finally, feeling dirty and sick, the men were done. The boss grabbed the child from his father and told the woman to take the child and clean herself up.

As she left, she heard the man speak one last time: "Don't come to me for your supply anymore. You're a cokehead and you're snorting more product than you sell. If you cross my path again, my friends will do to you what they did to your bitch. Do you understand?"

"Yeah… I mean, yes, I understand," he responded as even more tears fell from his eyes.

"Why do drug addicts always need to have the people in their lives fucked up in order to learn to stop fucking up? What do you think, Jam?"

The enforcer spoke up. "I don't know, boss. But that shit looked like it hurt his girl's asshole!"

They both laughed as the boss dropped his cigar to the living floor and left it there to burn a hole in the cheap rug. The boss paused and stayed for a moment longer, turning and looking the weeping man in the face.

"Look at me. Your drug selling privileges in this town are over!" He glared at the man one last time. "You're done here. And now, we're done."

The man sat in shock as all the men left. Too embarrassed to comfort his girl, he sat there and got drunk and high with what he had left. For the next few weeks, he tried to be a decent person, but then the woman came up pregnant. He knew the child could not be his. He stayed as long as he could. But being there was also being drunk, belligerent, and abusive. He took his anger and embarrassment out on the woman that had paid his penance for stealing drugs, and all he gave her was grief until the day he woke up, went to get cigarettes, and never came back.

She hadn't been in a relationship since he left—she would never trust a man again, ever. Strangely, she would meet a violent end at the hands of the man that taught her to hate men.

In the years that followed his exit, the once fit young bad boy became a shell of himself.

His liver was gone from all the drinking, so he was jaundiced in his eyes and skin. He weighed just north of 120 pounds—between the drinking and drugs, he didn't often find time to eat. The night it happened; the twins and the boy were all asleep in the room they shared. Their mother, who had been selling herself to make ends meet, was ushering out the last man of the evening.

At the end of each night, she rubbed herself down in a steaming shower and cried. She had no one to lean on—her family had not spoken to her since she left school. She hated every man that came to see her. Some of them really liked her, but she only saw them as money for food and clothes for her children.

Some of them were just out to feel like men again. Whatever the reason, they showed up and continued to pay her.

It was 1982, the last night the children would have a mother. The man had come over and gently knocked on the door. It caught her off guard; she wasn't expecting another customer, and she had already showered. She was in a nightgown and robe, tired, and just wanted to go to bed. For some reason, she slipped on her house shoes and shuffled her way to the door. As she prepared to answer it, she absently pushed a few strands of hair from her face and took a breath ready to tell the person on the other side of the door that she was done for the night.

She lay on her back, choking on her own blood and staring up at the first and only man she had ever loved. Why did she answer that door? That question was one of her final thoughts as the man that had fathered her first child barged in and began choking her in the doorway. She never made a sound; she couldn't speak or breathe. The door hung open, and her house shoes lay askew where he had picked her up off her feet. He dragged her into the bedroom and threw her to the floor, then gathered himself and put a boot to her face—he didn't want to wake the kids. She spit out her teeth and was about to yell when he dropped down onto her stomach and began to pummel her face and chest. She was left unrecognizable, gurgling blood, and staring up at the last person she would ever see.

He stood up slowly. It all happened so fast; he had wanted to speak to her but lost it the moment he saw her. He had wanted to ask her if he could come home, to tell her that he was sorry for everything that had happened. But the blank look on her face and the fear in her eyes set him off. In the end, he loved her more than anyone would ever know. He sat down and leaned against the woman's bed. He would give the police no motive. It wasn't hard to know what had happened, and he'd left plenty of evidence. He stood, walked over to the phone on the nightstand, and slowly dialed 911.

He told them that his girlfriend was dead and the killer was still there. He hung up the phone and walked to where she lay lifeless. He crumbled to the ground. What had he just done? She had been the love of his life and the mother of his son. It was that look when she answered the door. He didn't see love; she looked shocked. So, his chemically altered brain thought she was angry, and he just couldn't take it. When police arrived onsite, he was sitting there staring at the lifeless woman and his bloody fists. When they yelled for him to show his hands, he raised them high and told them there were three children in the second bedroom and to please not let them see this.

The man pled guilty to murder in the first.

He would never see another free day in his

life. No one spoke on his behalf, and he was

convicted, sentenced, and sent away quickly.

Within two years, he died of an overdose while

sitting in a maximum-security prison in Texas.

He never told any cellmates, his court-

appointed attorneys, or the guards why he did

what he did. It was the moment in time that he

took to the grave. As he lay there struggling to

breathe his last few gasps, he began to weep.

For the first time in his adult life, he prayed. If

there was a Hell, he would surely end up there,

but in his last thoughts he prayed that he might

be with the woman for eternity. He would beg

for her forgiveness and tell her that he had

gone there to ask her to take him back. The last

bit of air that escaped his body released him—

not absolving him but allowing him to be free

of guilt. The last words he spoke were,

"Love… I loved her."

The children, as this new journey began,

were just told that their mother had passed

away. They were never allowed to enter or see

the bedroom. No family (grandparents or aunts

or uncles) had asked to take them. *No one*

asked to take them. The boy, not knowing any

better, asked why his dad couldn't take them.

Not one official of the state had an answer

other than that his dad was not available. The

lie allowed the young man to keep Dad as a

hero. And all that time, he wondered why he

wouldn't just call. Dad would come for the three of them if he knew they needed him. It's those lies that children tell themselves about their parents that perpetuate the idea that once a person becomes a parent, they are better than whatever they had been before.

So, the children went from foster home to foster home, and they were kept together until the twins were adopted. The older child, though, would age out of foster care. When he aged out, the only thing he'd tell himself was that she left him. The young man would spend his life angry at his mother for dying. He thought that she probably had OD'd in her bedroom all those years ago. She left him to be screwed over by the system. *Fuck the twins*, he thought. He didn't know where they went, and he would never speak to them again. *They would have the perfect life*, he thought. *But me? What did the world give me? Nothing. You make your own way in the world.*

As he finished up his time in the foster care system, his case worker finally told him that his mother had been murdered. It shocked him; for once in his life he felt something different for his mother. In that moment, he didn't hate her. He asked what had happened. As he was now an adult, they told him the truth, that his father had… *Father* was the last word he heard. It's not that he stopped listening, he just couldn't comprehend another word of the conversation. He left confused, and it would be months before he'd get even close to being okay with what he'd learned.

Back in 1978, Christmas morning, and he was in his room. *Dad must have carried me in! I can't believe I fell asleep.* The boy hopped out of bed and ran to the kitchen. "Dad?!" he yelled as he entered the kitchen.

"Honey, sit down," his mother, stifling tears but attempting to be cheerful about the upcoming morning, said to him. "Your dad couldn't make it in yesterday. I'm sorry, but when your brother and sister wake up, you all have presents to open. Merry Chri—"

"What did you do?" he angrily yelled at his mother, "He said he would be here! You pissed him off again! Why?"

"I didn't do anything. Look, son, your dad wanted to be here, but—" She paused. What did she say here? *He's a junkie and wino, he'll never keep a promise to you or anyone*? She decided to protect him, as usual.

"Your dad wanted to be here, but he couldn't make it. He wasn't able to make it into town today," she said feebly, failing to tell her son the truth about his father for another missed visit.

She would never know how the boy that she protected from learning the truth about his father, whom he idolized, would harbor hate for his mother until the day that she died. She would never know that the boy would become a hate-filled man that considered his mother's death and his father's subsequent imprisonment all her fault.

Upon learning everything that had happened, he tried to understand. He wanted it all to make sense. Why would his father do such a thing? *Not Dad*, he thought. Until it finally made sense to him: It had been her fault.

As an adult, he would tell himself, "She just kept pushing! Dumb bitch got what she had coming." For this insomniac, his reality would always be that a woman that ruined his life and the life of the man—his father-- that she kept away from him. She kept his dad away from him. When days turned into weeks, and he wasn't sleeping, the ideas became darker. His truth became quite a bit slanted. He liked the dark…

He suddenly snaps back to the present moment in his dingy apartment. He has a love-hate relationship with living. Most of his life, he has wanted to die. As an adult, he has attempted suicide many times. He remembers that as a teen he'd heard that if you commit suicide, you go to Hell. Going to Hell seemed scary to him as a sixteen- or seventeen-year-old kid. He never went to church—that was for weak-minded followers, sheep. No, he picked up his ideas over time. So, going to Hell: Bad! And what gives you an express ticket? Suicide.

God couldn't be happy seeing me suffer, right? Alive, depressed, and angry, but why would God let him suffer? He finally accepted, somewhere along the way, that God must be a woman—only a woman would make you hang on with no hope and no escape.

The lights of the city pour in like a cold shower. It stings his senses that so much light can come through his dirty windows. The reds, greens, blues, and every other piece of the rainbow feel…cold. Night after night, he sits there staring at all the colors, but he's never quite figured out how it makes him feel. He would slice his hands through the different shades and stare at the colors on his pale skin. Staring directly out the windows at the light stings his eyes like the needles of water that hit you when you get into a too cold shower. It puts your entire body on alert, each hair follicle standing at attention, and you have to let out an audible howl that feels more like a reboot. For an instant, everything makes you take a deep breath while your body tells you what is happening. The same thing happens to him each night when the night light hits his eyes. The sting, the pain, the sharp breath, and the short howl. Then he can sit and listen to the night.

Listening to the night was the thing that kept him from ledges. The sound of humans and the outside world, with no interaction. When he was younger, he had been a people watcher. He loved to sit in a mall or on a park bench and just casually stare. He didn't feel like he was being creepy, but he'd been called

a creep more times than he cared to remember.

So, night after night, he sits by the window

with the broken green blinds. He can close it

all the way; well, almost. The last guy that

lived here must have been nosy—the blinds

are bent to shit. The insomniac wonders what

that person was looking for through the blinds.

Did they ever find it?

The insomniac doesn't look through the

window. His back is to the window and wall,

and he sits crisscross-apple sauce on his filthy

floor.

Crisscross-apple sauce? He hadn't thought

of that saying for a long time. He chuckles as

he stares at the lights bouncing off the floor.

He slowly moves his hands through the beams of light and begins to wonder what time he had come to. He stares at an empty wrist and thinks, *It's skin o'clock*. Another term from when he was a kid. But "skin-o'clock" is really just another way of saying it's getting really late. And things are about to pick up.

So, we're creeping deeper and deeper into the night. He has some work that he could do. Contract work, all from the comfort of his table. Since the world shut down a couple years ago, it didn't look or sound strange that he wanted to work from home. People delivered groceries, meals from restaurants, his mail… He never had to leave. Every purchase or paid bill is taken care of with his online accounts, where his paycheck is sent every two weeks.

He lights a cheap cigarette. It's not for the taste—cigarettes and smokers smell dirty, that stale funky smell that permeates your hair and clothes. No, he smokes for the rush he feels when he takes the first drag. The loose feeling of his mind and the cool that sweeps through his chest. Sure, he's done drugs, but cigarettes are just for a momentary legal buzz. He took a drag from the only vice he still had. It's funny, in his mind at least quitting the drugs and booze gave him an agoraphobic complex. Being sober had given him complete disdain for people of all shades and makes and models. He laughs, takes another drag, feeling his momentary high… His eyes move to the music of those lights. It's a tune that only he hears; really, he believes the insomniacs in the deep water all hear music that the lights beam out each night. He feels safe in this desperate hour, but his mind will never really allow him to let his guard down.

He glances at the ceiling. Sometimes it floats away. How many days has it been? How long can a person last without sleep? He'd look it up, but he honestly doesn't give a shit about how much longer he will be here. The lights do their dance, the cigarette does its job, and the insomniac does *his* job and stays awake. Again.

Part 2:

"It's 4:30 a.m. on a Tuesday—it doesn't get much worse than this."

Adam Duritz (Counting Crows), "Perfect Blue Buildings"

As the night moves into the darkest hours, the insomniac begins to travel backward in his mind, first just a couple years, then a decade. In the beginning, he ponders on the past few relationships he'd been able to find in his wreck of a life. He thought it was sad that when you're an outsider in the high school world, you attract two types of people: the clean-cut good kids looking for drugs, and outsiders like yourself. In his life, he had found it was mostly the outsiders that found spending any time with him was worthwhile. So, walking that path during the long hours sometimes soothed him, but what chick would take him down that road tonight?

Tonight, who would he think of? Would it

be a conquest or one of the times his heart had been broken? *Funny thing*, he thought as he took another first drag from the cigarette, *heartbreaks and conquests often go hand in hand.* Men of all ages seem to think they have some control in the conquest of a woman. The facts, as a man sees them: a woman wants them, they are willing to put out for them, thus the woman is the sacrifice to the man. But what really happens is that once the man has been with that woman, the dynamics completely change, and the woman is now in control of when and where the sex happens. The man goes from conqueror to conquest. Because of that violent shift, men quickly become the underdogs in any relationship or sexual arrangement. Now he has become a snatch-fiend, and he will chase any woman— *any* woman—to get his fix. Crawling, scraping, and paying to get what he now yearns for every minute of every day.

The insomniac leans against the windowsill; he blows smoke down toward the opening at the bottom. The smoke billows up from the opening and creates a small cloud. If it were a cartoon, this cloud would show his thoughts. In this instant, though, it's a time-travel cloud. He's sixteen, he knows about sex from magazines he found and videos at some parties. He has cum a million times on his stomach; sometimes wipes it up, but most often falls asleep and wakes up with crusty sheets and a crusty stomach. He thinks it would be fun to try it with an actual girl, but truthfully, he doesn't know how to talk to girls, much less approach them about sex. It's the 80s—the internet is a decade away and porn is much harder to come by. They keep the good stuff behind the counter at gas stations, and all the foster homes he's lived in have a lot of church stuff all over the house, so finding porn there is a lost cause.

The insomniac on the ledge giggles at the phrase. *A lost cause?* The thought makes him giggle every time it crosses his mind. The childish giggle of a person you see and hear in a public place and know something is not quite right with them. More than one bimbo has called him an asshole over the years. It was sometimes the giggling, or the way he hyper-focused on people when he was in public. He knew that he did this, the staring at people, but he didn't care what people thought. Never had he cared what anyone thought of him, how he dressed, or how he spoke. Life was about mental freedom, about trying to find his way with no family. It's his personal belief that he's better off without his mother or the twins—less baggage—but he still misses his dad every day. Besides, he enjoys his hobby, he even has a name for it: people- watching. It's his only consistent hobby, other than masturbating (yet another giggle escapes). During the day, he would go places like parks and malls. The parks are not typically the best, as parents would think he was staring at kids. And he knew one thing: staring at kids, well, that's fucking sick shit. The sickest thing one could be is a pedo. It's the worst thing anyone could do. So no, he didn't stare at children.

The moms though? The moms were prime staring material. If they're a mom—and this always made sense to him—they had at least put out for the children's father, and chances were good that they'd do it again. So, staring didn't get him any women during the day. But at night…well, the night is a different world. The people on the city streets after midnight are hoping to get looked at, stared at, maybe find a fun night. His thing was to sneak out his bedroom window—the Bible-thumpers typically went to bed by 9:30 and never checked on him or any of the other kids.

In cheap tennis shoes, hand-me-down blue jeans, and a rock band t-shirt, he'd make his way downtown toward the places where his kind of people roamed. There were three types down there: the three P's. Pimps, prostitutes, and prey. The first night he was out there, looking at the brashly dressed women with stiletto heels, mini-skirts, and tube-tops, it was a lot for him. The pimps, they set up shop near the women and were easy to spot. A nice car and a suit. Some suits nicer than others, some as outlandish as the little bit of clothing worn by the women who worked for them.

One thing the boy learned quickly: pimps don't like gawkers hanging around. Their business is about productivity. And women standing along the street getting stared at doesn't make money. The first few nights, the boy had been unceremoniously moved from the area. One pimp or another had informed him that it wasn't a peep show, and he'd do well to scram. It took a bit to find the areas where he could do his looking. At first, watching the whores and the lowlifes walking the streets was enough. He would skulk back to his bedroom, rub one out real quick, and get to sleep. But once you've seen the women leaning into the cars a few times, you realize that most of them (for convenience) had nothing on underneath. It made him want one of those women in the worst way. Thus began his career as a pickpocket and a thief.

At first, he wasn't very good. With no one to teach him, he had gotten slapped around a few times. He was determined though, and soon he was lifting wallets and watches. The best time to go into the pawn shops that would buy his type of goods was at night. In the city, you can find anything at night. He would sell what he could, save some money, and the rest he'd spend with the women on the streets. They knew he was a kid, they called him a kid, but no one cared as long as his money was green.

So, from staring, to stealing, and then to

getting laid. He liked the city life, the colors, the raw smell of the night. Yeah, this was his type of place. And the longer he was there, the more people came to know him as Kid. In that world, no one knows your real name, who you are, if you have a family or kids. That life is all about the now. What can you do for me right now? He had become a street rat. People knew he was the kid to go to for watches, rings, and other fancy stuff that people wore to the wrong places. And what he didn't fence on the street, he went to his favorite pawn shops to haggle for a good price.

Staring through the dirty window, not caring about the time, the man stares deep into the night. He remembers that he first started sleeping less and less in his 17th and 18th years. As long as he arrived home before sun-up, they were none the wiser. He found a place to hide stolen goods, money, and drugs. The Bible-thumpers glanced in each child's room once, maybe twice, per week. If it looked clean, they would never step inside. He knew that a good appearance creates apathy in the supervisors of the world. This would serve him well later. Look good and the world will always think you are good.

On the streets, Kid would sometimes get free pussy or head in exchange for jewelry. The pimps didn't like that, but if they got their proper amount at the end of the night, they didn't give a fuck where it came from.

Kid found that certain girls partied harder than others. He liked the girls that were way out there, they knew how to have fun. The longer he walked the streets, the more he realized certain truths. One: these people were not bad people to him. After a time, you see beyond the streets, and you see that everyone looks out for the other night people. And two: he hated paying for sex, but a man's gotta do what a man's gotta do! And that caused him to giggle again. As the thoughts of hookers and soccer moms with nice bodies race through his head, he suddenly stops. Where does he really want to go?

Ah yes, sixteen. He had recently started walking the city streets through the night, and he knew a thing or two now. To the night

people of the city, yeah, he still looked and

acted like a kid. In this little suburb, during the

day, he looked like a dangerous man. So, with

that, her name was Nicole. They had been in

the same classes through elementary school

and junior high. But in high school, the smart

kids do smart things, and guys like him

retreated to the back of the room and stayed

quiet. Strangely enough, people think that the

loud, disrespectful, mean kids are hellraisers!

He called bullshit on that; being like that was a

kid attitude. He knew adults were the best

actors in the world. They hid their dark sides,

their loudness and quirks. Why? Because—

and he knew that if anything in the world was

true, this was it—bad people never want you to know how bad they are.

Loud people show their ignorance and immaturity to everyone. Think about it: How many serial killers have walked—and still do—the streets for years? Right there, under everyone's noses, never hiding and never scared. Why? Because clean and neat appearances create apathy from law and other authorities. It's simple. The people running around yelling, hitting random people, doing other public crimes—they aren't the people you should worry about. They get caught quickly, they cry and beg forgiveness, and they get beat up and fucked in prison.

No, the loud, rude, mean people are not the

dangerous people. They blow all the smoke to look tough and hope they never run into someone really dangerous that isn't fooled by their bravado.

So, no, he didn't act out in class, talk over the teacher, cut farts…none of that stuff. He drew pictures in his notebooks and squeaked by in each class by turning in an attempt at homework and just showing up.

Now, back to Nicole. He had been more aware of her since maybe eighth grade. Many times, it wasn't a body that he noticed when he was younger; no, it was an attitude. Attraction is quite hard to explain. No two people think the same thing when they see someone. Sure, there are the obviously beautiful and handsome people, but they are rare, and when they're young everybody wants to befriend them and date them. But to him, how a girl carried herself was what made her attractive. It wasn't until he got older and just wanted sex that the idea of finding an attractive woman didn't matter. Ugly, boring, sad women—they needed it too. And on those after-midnight strolls, he found those women from time to time. Not pros, just hoes! He giggled at that very thought.

He's distracted tonight, he wants to think about Nicole. It had been both of their first times. In the back of her mom's car. She was popular, known in town, and a cheerleader, so the Bible-thumpers had no problem with her picking him up to help him study. It was about 5:30 in the afternoon on a Thursday in the fall. Right in the middle of football season. Her friends would be at the game. It was the junior varsity games tonight, and she cheered on Friday nights.

The entire ordeal was surreal. He was uncomfortable, the rolled-up windows were foggy, and the car had gotten really warm inside as their breathing rhythms increased. He was still sort of new with his midnight strolls and had only gotten head since it cost about $10. Since he liked it, and wasn't yet the thief that he would become, he never saved the money to get laid. So, yes, Nicole was his first time in a woman.

He was nervous. He was a quiet and dangerous guy, and this girl was a cute virgin. The first thing he noticed as they undressed was her smell. She smelled exquisite, like a dream really. She was soft and had a nicely landscaped area down below. From what he knew, she might not be ready. He clumsily began kissing her neck and chest all the while his hand awkwardly mashed her vagina in an uncomfortable way. She was a trooper though. She didn't say anything so as not to embarrass him. He'd seen enough porn to know that he should eat her next. Strangely, this was his favorite part. No other time in his life did he like it. She was an unspoiled flower, and her warmth and moistness were so satisfying. She gently moaned; ironically, it crossed both their minds at the same time that he had done something right. He knew it was time when she relaxed her legs from around his head. He sat up, stared her in the eyes, and moved forward.

"Do you have a…" She was embarrassed to ask.

"Oh, yeah, I do have one," he said nervously. He reached toward his back pocket, pulled out a tattered Velcro wallet, and pulled out a condom. This was his first time trying to use a condom—he started to put it on, but then noticed he'd put the wet side toward the inside, and he knew that didn't seem right. He quickly turned it around and slid it on himself.

He didn't get it in the right spot the first try. He said, "Sorry about that," and backed up to try again. This time it worked, but he was even more nervous now that it had started.

"Owww. It hurts," she whispered to him.

"Do you want me to stop?"

"No, please don't stop."

They continued for what seemed like just a moment but was about seven minutes. She squeezed his shoulders as she was getting close to finishing. Never having done this before, she didn't know how much longer it would last, but it felt better each time he moved in and out.

Then he suddenly thrusted in heavily and squeezed her back as he finished. She felt the condom move a bit and knew what was happening, but it was just an unbelievable moment.

As they separated from one another, he sat back, breathing heavily. They stared at one another awkwardly for a moment. Leaning against the doors, they quietly spoke for a moment or so. She then made the move to say it was time for her to go home.

Then came getting dressed, the time to feel strange, sleepy, and hungry. She looked embarrassed for a moment as they noticed she had left blood on the seat (the seats were leather, so that was easy to clean up). They quietly dressed, no cuddling or sweet talk, just the very quiet ride home and the awkward goodnight kiss on the cheek. And then they parted company as lovers for the first and only time.

How it ended up happening is still a mystery to him. Even to this day, night after night as he crept through the dark, he would think of her. Every time he thought of her and that night, he wondered how it had started.

The first time they had ever spoken was that week, Monday morning. She was late and had to take a seat at the back of the classroom next to—guess who—yeah, our guy. He had been invisible throughout his school days. Then, in one instant, someone had seen him.

A slight smile from the girl. He felt queasy

for a moment; he wanted to stare but he fought it and just smiled back and began drawing again. She quietly asked him what he was drawing. Again, that feeling in the pit of his stomach; he'd heard of butterflies in the stomach, but he'd never had them before. People, much less girls, never talked to him…ever.

He takes a long drag from his cigarette, and it does its job. He's calming down, but when he thinks of the time so long ago in that backseat, he purses the cigarette tightly between his lips. With his now-free hands, he makes a move toward his pants. The perfect world of teen sex…awkwardness, pain, the uncontrollable urge to go as fast as possible (in case she tried to change her mind). All that and the afterglow. Yes, the afterglow as a teenager was quite amazing. No matter the moment; in the end, all awkwardness, shyness, pain, sorrow, anger, and sadness escaped and lay inside the condom he'd clumsily put on minutes earlier.

They spoke after the glow ended. It was quiet, it was warm, and they were each leaning against the doors that hid them in the back of that car. He had recorded the entire conversation in his memory. This was, to him, the only time he had ever acted like a person with love in his heart. And, well, it ended abruptly when she said, "I have to go home."

After dressing, they moved to the front seat

and began the quiet trip home. As she stopped the car, he leaned over and gave an awkward one-sided kiss.

"Nicole, will I see you again?" he remembers asking as they stopped in front of the house where he lived. He would never let his guard down again after the following moment…

"I'll see you in class." Now her speech felt cold and distant. She couldn't even look at him.

He takes a swallow—yes, it was weakness. He wanted to cry, but he asked the only thing left to ask. "I mean, will I see you like thi—".

Nicole cut him off. "No, we can never do is

again. It's nothing you did, we just can't."

And that was it. Nothing else to say, nothing else would be said by her. She sat quietly and looked forward as a sign that it was time for him to leave. From that Monday morning to that Thursday morning, she sat next to him. They spoke about things he liked to draw, she shared things about what it was like to be a cheerleader, and they shared laughs about some of the other people in the classroom.

Only in first period had they spoken. That Thursday afternoon, he was beginning to walk home. He heard her sweet voice and looked over his left shoulder. She was driving by and asked if he could use a ride home.

"Sure, thanks," he replied as he hopped in the car. "What are you doing tonight?"

"Me? I just hang out at home. Every night. Why?" Beginning and ending with a question hit him as strange, but sitting here in her car was nothing but strange.

"Would you like to hang out with me?" With a wistful look and a half-smile, she had control of him.

"Sure. But my foster parents might not like it. I can tell them that you're helping me with schoolwork. If that's okay with you?"

"How about I come by to pick you up at

5:30?" She gave him a long stare, and she bit the corner of her lip in only the way a beautiful woman that has her hooks in you knows how to do.

He didn't know what all this meant, but he felt a bit sick to his stomach as he agreed. They pulled up to the house and he hopped out. He looked back as she drove away. Could she really like him? Would she show back up later? As a teenage boy his biggest thought was, "Why me?"

He went upstairs and calmly gathered himself. He lifted his small, stiff mattress and grabbed a condom—maybe he wouldn't need it, but if things went well with Nicole, he would use his first condom.

He sat down for dinner with the huge foster family. The Bible-thumpers always asked everyone about their day. What did you learn? Who did you meet? Do you have homework? Any plans for the weekend?

Being the oldest kid there, he always stayed close to the vest. This day, he started by asking if he might go study with a friend that evening.

With a shocked expression, Mr. Rivers asked, "You have a friend? I'm glad to hear that.

"Who are you studying with?" Mrs. Rivers dabbed her mouth a cloth napkin as she spoke.

"Umm, her name is Nicole Meyers."

"The cheerleader?" exclaimed Mrs. Rivers

"Yes, ma'am," the boy said.

"You know her, Nelson. The young lady is one of the youth leaders at the church on the other side of town. Yes, that would be a wonderful use of your time. If you agree, Nelson?"

Mr. Rivers put down his fork and stared at his wife, and spoke up, "Sure, Michelle." Then to the boy, "You know, that sounds like a good move on your part."

"Thank you," he said as he finished dinner and sat waiting for 5:30 to come while listening to all the other children talk about their day.

He grabbed his backpack and walked out when Nicole arrived. Looking over his shoulder, he waved bye to the children on the porch.

After he had arrived back home and gone to his room, the thoughts started darting across his mind. Why him? Was it a joke or a bet? No, he decided that it was sincere, but the reality of being with this guy hit a bit different after sex. It finally hit him as to why she chose this day— her friends would be at the game. They had gone somewhere he had never been… Had she been there before? With another guy? And at the end of it all, she never sat next to him, spoke to him, or acknowledged him in any way again.

And this was the end of his being an open person, a loving person, and any chance of ever caring for anyone again. The blank stare on her face hurt more than anything else that she could have chosen to do.

Hands in pockets as deep as they could go, shoulders hunched making him look like he was cold, the last word he ever spoke to her was, "Thanks."

The anger burns just as much so many years later. Yet, every time he walks that path in his mind, he ends up masturbating to the memory. He wonders if anyone sees him jacking off in his window to the lights of the night and the glow of his cigarette. He grips himself and goes ever faster as the story ends in his mind. The way she couldn't look at him as they cleaned up or as he left. When he saw her at school for the next year, she looked away—every fucking time. He thought, *If I could just get her to look at me…* But she never did—not once. He left school early; he decided he wasn't getting anything from just sitting there drawing pictures.

He would get a GED, take some online courses, and move to the city. He would work dead-end jobs while completing school. The jobs, along with financial aid, would pay for rent, food, and school. It was in the city, so he didn't need a car. And at night he was Kid, and he would make extra money with his nefarious dealings. He was a great pickpocket these days, and he would frequent the same women throughout the week. He rarely slept, even then. By the late 90s, he had money put aside from selling stolen goods and hustling on the streets. But he knew he was getting too old to just be Kid to everyone. So, he became interested in computers and this thing known as the internet. He learned about computers and found work with them. First was simple programming. Then he realized he had a knack for this stuff, so he learned photo and video editing, audio mastering, and other things he could do from home.

He would be in demand for his skills but using him came at the price of doing everything online. So, he found a company that he contracted with, and customers

followed. He became a reclusive remote

worker. He was good at what he did. He didn't

ever join meetings with his camera, and he

liked how it felt. A hired gun, he went to the

highest bidder. He worked at his own pace,

which he considered the speed of life. Fuck the

speed of business, people who work by the

hour pad their hours to get more money. He

was paid by the job, and he did quality work at

a great pace. And he did things on his own

hours.

So even now, he loves the nights. The

insomniac lives his dreams. Nobody knows

him when he's out cruising for trim, and being

a hired gun allows him to buy some when he

wants it. In this new day of websites and apps for finding anything you want, you can get whores online, but it's the night and the hunt as he stalked the streets that he enjoys… He laughs at this when he thinks of cruising the late-night streets; yes, he laughs his giggle.

With a quiet grunt, he finishes. He almost bit through his cigarette this time. He has filthy stomach hairs matted with cum. He lowers his shirt and cleans up a bit, closes his pants, and moves into the darkness of his apartment. He feels lost for a moment. He had started crying while he was finishing; that was new. He didn't cry. Not him. This angers him, then the thought crosses his mind.

It's dark. At about three or four in the

morning, the night is at its darkest. Thus, the phrase, "darkest before dawn." Yes, the darkest moments, where only the vile are on the streets. He'd once been told that the only things on the streets after 1 a.m. are dogs and men.

Yeah, he understands that and lives it. He's not a nice person in the late hours. He keeps his skills as a pickpocket sharp, and the women still working are the desperate ones. The ones with kids being raised by grandparents while the mother is out getting plowed for some coke or meth. He typically looks for these women; they work hard for their cash. He personally likes their effort, but he always makes sure to wear a condom. The

sins born in these hours are those that burn into
your heart. He has seen junkies OD and lay
there in an alley for days, hookers squatting
down when a condom had broken and
bouncing up and down trying to get rid of the
chance of a kid, and married older closeted
men looking for young men to give them
favors before returning home to a wife that no
longer satisfies them and coaching their kid's
baseball team while secretly thinking of the
young men they spent their money on during
those late nights on the city's streets.

Eventually, those sins find the day. One
day, the wife finds used condoms under the
seat, her husband's bloody underwear, or a
picture that he decided to take of his guy

friend. At first, she'll ignore it. Then he keeps going out and keeps going out, more and more often. And like a volcano, it all overflows. Closet queens ruin their homes, their kids grow up hating their dads because they left Mom for a man. At least the guys that hire women leave with a bit of self- respect. And these days, you never know what might be under their dress, so the insomniac may deviate from one woman to another, but he tries to stay with women he knows. It can really be a jungle out there in the late hours. You can get robbed, shot, or find a hooker with a bigger cock than you. Life's a bitch, right?

As he wanders around his apartment, he

wonders what life is really about. After all these years, he has nothing outside of this dingy apartment to show that he even exists. Being invisible has its perks. Being invisible is his way of existing. But the darkest hour is ending. Another night is about to pass. He had come up with an idea recently, a way to stay invisible even at 5 a.m. and the light of morning begins to butt its way into his night. He wants to try the insomniac's lullaby.

The insomniac's lullaby is an idea he had thought of many years ago. On one of those painful and unhappy nights, he found he was nearing the end of his rope, and there would be no fooling God if he let go of that rope. But that could send him to sleep; he could finally sleep. The insomniac's lullaby was his solution.

How do you put an insomniac to sleep? This was his thought, and it puzzled him. He'd gone online and looked for ways to cure his insomnia. So many quacks out there with different ideas. Weed, melatonin, and pills were the most popular ones of course. Then there were ideas like meditation, something called valerian root, magnesium, even lavender. His favorite had been exercise followed by a warm glass of milk.

But the deeper down the rabbit hole you go, the more interesting the ideas get. And sooner or later, you find an idea for the solution that's even better than the problem.

Oh yes, you can find anything on the internet.

So, hours later, far beyond lavender and

melatonin, he found a page called *The

Soldier's Guide to Sleep: The Insomniac's

Lullaby*. The actual site had a witty name like

sleepinsomniac.com. Either way, this was the

bottom of the insomnia rabbit hole.

Nothing more to look for, no more digging;

this page had the best solution he had found.

He burned it into his memory and hoped to use

it when he could no longer stand another

sleepless night, when the insomnia had

become too much. He had been awake for so

long that reality now mixed with those twilight

moments where you aren't sure if the world is

still real. His moments now intermingled like a

large group of kids at a playground, he wasn't sure. But he was finally at the end of the rope; he needed sleep.

There were a couple steps when beginning the Insomniac's Lullaby:

"First, you must be in the darkest hours, at the very end of the night. It called for the participant to be in the shadows, where no one can see and interfere. Now, you must remember that eyes from street cameras, police cameras, phones, and other insomniacs are always watching. The proper way to begin is to be in your home, a comfortable and familiar place where you may begin to relax.

Second, you pick a song. The

instructions there were sketchy, but the one

thing it encouraged was that it preferably

be one that is loud. The writer reiterates

that it sounds counterintuitive, but it works

best this way.

And the finisher after this poetic

set-up? He smiled widely, got a cigarette

from the pack to get that first drag feeling

again; as he released the smoke, he felt

that little lift hit his brain.

The finisher, well, that is the big mystery.

No one has ever recorded the answer

which he needs."

But does it work? Staring at the clock, the

man decides there's really only one way to

find out.

He walks to the old stereo and lifts the lid, grabs a lint brush, and begins to clean the turntable. When he's satisfied that it's ready, he digs through his vinyl records and pulls out the perfect album with the perfect song. Audioslave's 2002 self-titled album. To him, the magnum opus is "I Am the Highway." He takes the record out and stares at it for just a brief moment. He blows the lint and dust from the record. Like a purveyor of fine art, he takes his time, inspecting both sides of the record to ensure it's in perfect condition. Next, he moves to the turntable on the desk. He has wiped it down, so he knows it's ready to go. He places the record on the turntable but doesn't immediately start it up. He stares down at the record and just thinks…

Yes, Chris Cornell was a genius. A beautiful soul, with a world of words to share. He left us too soon. It's sad poetry in his mind. He continues to stare at the record, and instinctively he pushes the power button. He hears the hum of the amplifier. Then he finds his song and turns it up.

The darkest hour is almost over, as is his journey. This long, fucked up journey. Without his dad, his mom, or his siblings. Yep, all of them had taken a piss on him. No one knows him and, guess what, they never will. They didn't care to know him for all his life up to this point. He only ever shared intimacy with one woman—Nicole. Otherwise, it was whores and horny housewives looking for fun in the city. He loved no one, nothing, and held loyalty to no one.

The truth is, he had always been alone. Alone is the way that he had lived. An entire life. It had been shit, a deep pile of shit. He is a horny, perverted creep that stares at people and has never really known love. Yes, he is awkward, angry, and lonely. Lonely—that's the one that hits him hardest. No matter how many things you put your dick in, it never really stops the loneliness when you don't know what love is.

He truly knows, deep down, that nothing in this world would let him sleep. He wonders again, as the music begins to play, *How long has it been since I slept?* How long can you live with no sleep? He lets out his giggle, that same fucking giggle he'd had his entire life, and has a clear and sobering thought—not for much longer. Not much longer at all. He leans his head back and lets the haunting voice of Chris Cornell sing him to sleep.

Epilogue:

"Long and weary my road has been... I am not your blowing wind—I am the highway."

Chris Cornell (Audioslave), "I Am the Highway"

"It was the smell. I mean, that's why I called," the man's neighbor said to the uniformed police officers in the hallway. The crime scene investigators arrived in the dingy apartment building and dressed to begin working the scene: sanitized gloves and shoe coverings, along with head coverings and coveralls to avoid contaminating the scene. They had gone into the apartment to secure the scene, get evidence samples, and do a quick inspection of the immediate area. At this juncture, it was straightforward—uniforms kept the looky-loos away, the crime scene investigators gathered physical evidence that would be used to piece together what had happened…and then there were the detectives.

At least two older detectives had been in and out of the apartment. Their immediate job was to look for clues that might indicate manner and motives of death. The men, late 40s, wore polyester suits, and at least one of them had a clip-on tie. Neither man looked as if they worried or cared about their health or appearance. They had long since lost their love and sense of adventure with the job; it was now just another day at the office. One thing, though, was that the stench was overwhelming. The detectives gave each other a knowing look as they prepared to enter the apartment; that smell is something an officer never really gets used to. As the scene investigators arrived, they saw Detective Clip-On losing what had not digested of his chili dog lunch. He had made it to the hallway and ran into the first crime scene investigator on site.

"Thanks for preserving the crime scene, Davis," he said with a laugh.

"Yeah, ha-ha," replied Detective Davis. The investigator could have sworn on the stand that Detective Davis was green when they met in the hallway.

"Dirty job, but someone's gotta do it—right, Detective?"

While wiping his mouth with an old handkerchief from his right hip pocket, the detective thought to himself, *"Fucking crime scene investigators are assholes"*, then continued to wipe his mouth of bits of chili dog.

"Go do your job!" he yelled at the investigator. The investigator just laughed it off, threw the detective a half-hearted salute, and continued laughing as he entered the dirty apartment.

The uniformed officers continued their investigations of the neighbors up and down the hallway.

"Didn't ever see him," a tall, skinny young man said first. The young man had short, curly brown hair and only wore pajama bottoms. "Hell, nobody would have known if he hadn't started stinking!"

"Every day, there were deliveries from

restaurants. Christ, he never left that apartment. The guy probably weighed a million pounds," a heavyset, judgy college girl said to the officers. It struck the uniformed officer that she probably weighed a million pounds herself. She was staring and talking to anyone who would listen, all the while eating a bagel slathered in cream cheese and a ton of strawberry preserves. To get in on the action, she had come out of her apartment in dirty, hole=filled pajamas with no bra under a faded *Class of '99* shirt. She tried her best, several times, to look into the apartment or get one of the uniformed officers to give her some information.

An older couple—a short, thin, grey-haired

woman standing next to a tall, slender, bald man—had stepped to the threshold of their own apartment, simply staring at the chaos as they stood in their doorway. "*So many years*", thought the husband, "*so many years, and in the last ten to fifteen this place has gone to hell*." He threw his hands up in disgust and walked back into his apartment. "*Let the looky-loos watch the sideshow*."

"This was a nice place then." he muttered to himself as he sat in an old cracked brown leather recliner.

In the apartment, the man had become bloated over the last week. As the police walked in, there was an eerie electric buzz coming from the stereo equipment. The record player and amp were still on, and the record was now motionless as the turntable's arm had returned to its seat after playing the final song on the record. The investigators were busying themselves with site photos and beginning to attempt to determine how long the insomniac had lain there.

The photographer, the quiet one of the group, stared at the apartment's curiosities. It was bare; save a twin bed, a desk with a very expensive computer, an old chair, a nice stereo, and a half-smoked pack of cigarettes. "Jesus, did he ever leave this place?" The apartment truly smelled of death…death, sweat, and stale cigarette smoke.

In those fleeting moments, as everyone

gawked and stared, the general milling about was starting to slow. The excitement was over; it was enough to have seen and smelled it… That would be enough for everyone on the floor to live on for a while. Nothing that exciting had happened in a long time.

In the waning moments of the clean-up, wandering amongst them—not seen, acknowledged, or heard—the essence of the insomniac was ready to leave. In life, he had been just as invisible to all these people. He didn't ever introduce himself, wave to anyone, or even knock on any of their doors.

The insomniac had been a lifelong loner. All of his adult life, he had needed no one. And he'd always taken pride in that. A self-made man: that's what he thought of himself. But never a man of the world. Had he ever wanted to be better? That was something that never truly bothered him. Sure, he would have liked to have seen and experienced more. But it was never meant to be. He would just be the guy that wasted his mind on sickness…always the sickness that came from his head.

He had been a woman-watching pervert that masturbated far too often. His talent with computers, that truly had been his calling. He was talented enough to be sought by companies all over the world. But would any of those companies have ever hired the real person he was in his heart and mind? He'd always known he was a very specific kind of person. A lonely, sad, angry man. He guessed that others would consider him a disturbed individual.

"Disturbed?" He thought that was a silly way to describe a person that needed help. His entire life boiled down to the fact that he needed help but didn't know how to ask, or even what, if anything, was wrong. He was just an individual. He'd heard that life was chess, not checkers, a marathon, not a foot race. What had he done in life that made any sense? Sure, his work was nice, but it wasn't living, was it? It had been an existence. A life wasted. No mom. No dad. No one.

A life wasted? Sure, maybe it had all been a life wasted. He had done what he wanted, right? He got laid with a lot of whores, a few free pieces of ass, and he was good at what he chose to do. The insomniac, for as much as he liked the depravity that constantly flooded his mind, had been a decent person. At least in his own mind.

But as he began to relax, in the moments after Chris Cornell had begun singing, the insomniac lived his entire life in a few brief moments. Do you have to think—or better yet, believe—that you were a decent person in life? This tidbit is what he pondered over more than any other thought in maybe his entire adult life.

"No Hell today, buddy," he had uttered in the waning moments of the dark hours. "No

Hell today? Buddy!"

In the end, he had thought about the Insomniac's Lullaby. The bottom of the rabbit hole; the place on the internet where you could dig no further. This idea had started during the Vietnam era. The site was interesting, but he found only one other mention of it anywhere. It was deep in the archives of a long-gone heavy metal magazine from the 80s. He'd heard of the magazine but never had the money to read it.

It was an interview with some singer; ten years later, that guy would be found with a crackpipe and an empty bottle of Jack beside him. The singer was asked about the coolest fact that he knew, and the story went like this:

"This is weird, don't think it's a fact for everyone," he started. "I had some friend that came back from Vietnam. When I say he was fucked up in the head, he was gone, man.

Anyways, we were having dinner. This is before the band, fame, really before everything happened for me. I was thinking I would be a failure as a musician and end up a plumber or something. Okay, so, we're getting on late into the night. We're sitting having drinks, and my friend begins telling me he's had insomnia for a while. He'd tried drugs and alcohol, but nothing had helped him. He told me that he had quit sleeping a month ago and would wander for hours throughout the night. This is where he got weird. In short, he was looking for something. That's when he first mentioned the phrase *Insomniac's Lullaby*. He says, 'I've decided to listen to the Insomniac's Lullaby.'"

It was here that the writer pointed out that the singer looked a bit spooked when he said it. So he had interrupted the man with the obvious question: "The Insomniac's Lullaby? What is that?"

The singer cleared his throat, took a drink of Jack, and spoke again. "I was getting there, man. He told me that in battle, they said not to worry about the shots you heard, because you never hear the bullet with your name on it. But he and

a group of his friends that had lost every

bit of their common sense as well made up

this lullaby to help them finally sleep."

The article mentioned that the singer

became more reflective in the

conversation; he was a bit shaken by the

memory of this story. The author mentions

that at this point, based on the look, he

asked if the man wanted to stop.

He was quiet for a moment but
declined to stop.

"The Insomniac's Lullaby was

simply the shot that you heard when you

were the one eating the bullet…" With this,

the singer gave a nervous laugh and

slugged back another shot of Jack. The article mentions that the singer's hand was trembling, but he continued.

"I thought it was all a joke. I began to laugh, so my friend joined in the laughter with me. We spoke for an hour or two longer, then he left. We lost contact after the band took off. I went home one weekend to visit my family. It was a couple years later. I had received a letter from him at my parents' home. It was short and to the point…"

It read:

Hey Man,

I've been reading about you. You made

it happen. I'm happy one of us is doing

something. I haven't slept in weeks, but it

feels like forever. I see what the guys

meant. I'm playing the Insomniac's

Lullaby tonight. I think I'll play one of

your songs on my way out…

Love you, Man.

The article continued:

> "It broke my heart. I scrambled to
> look back at the envelope. I needed to see
> the date on it. It arrived at my parents'
> home six months ago. I looked up his name
> in the back issues of our local paper. Yeah,
> six months earlier, my friend committed
> suicide. A single shot directly through the

roof of his mouth was the word on the street. So, yeah, it broke my heart, but then I couldn't help wondering which song he had picked."

The article finished with a bit about the upcoming release of the band's next album and to read each month for more fun facts.

The insomniac had loved that article when he found it, and read it over and over, he recalled, during his difficult times. But nothing makes you more desperate than feeling constantly on the edge and in a fog. Sleepy. Lost. Dazed. Not really knowing if it was day or night, what day it might even be. Yeah, it was the feeling of just floating about and feeling nauseous and dizzy at the same time. He had thought, *If I quit leaving the apartment, maybe I could finally get some sleep.* At least he hoped that would work for him. In the end, though, it changed nothing. It didn't help… Not one fucking bit…

The night was always so long. After not finding sleep for months or maybe longer, he was at the end of his rope. When you're alone, you realize that no one will reach down to pull you up when the rope has gotten short. It's you and the void that lies beneath. Is there sleep down there? He smiled at the thought of this.

His record player had been a source of pride and joy. He didn't have much else in the apartment. But just as in high school, he'd followed the rules. No loud music or booming TV. His computer speakers were always kept at a reasonable level. Yep, once again, he went under the radar. No one bothers you when you don't stick out. That had been his entire life. No one had cared for him. Not Mom or the twins. And in the end, he knew Dad was never a hero. His eyes teared up at this reality. He left. He had killed Mom. *Killed Mom.* Now he openly wept. Why had he been such a shit to her when she was alive? She deserved better.

He figured out a couple important things there at the brink of the lullaby. He was not a good or even decent person. He never was, and that made him stop crying. It was time for the rubber to hit the road, and he couldn't change anything. All the bravado of being a tough guy in life was gone now. No one would miss him. He realized that he had become the new three Ps in life: Pickpocket, pervert, and private.

He had pondered all this as he cleaned his turntable and looked through his albums for Audioslave. He took a moment to glance at the album cover. It was a double album, and he'd listened to the four sides many times over. But on this night, it was album two, side one. The first song was his favorite on this or any other album. "I Am the Highway" was hauntingly beautiful. So, he cleaned what little dust was on the record, placed it on the turntable, and pressed the start button. He briskly walked to his desk and reached in the upper right-hand drawer. There he kept the final item needed—a pistol. He'd always had it there, always loaded. And it was go time.

In the background, Chris Cornell's voice began to sing… It was his time now, and his song was just over five and a half minutes. In this moment, he thought of the one person that he had ever shown any type of affection to—Nicole. She was scared. He'd realized that a few years later. She was popular, smart, a churchgoing girl. He was an orphan, a nobody, and not known to be bright. In a small suburban town, hanging with the wrong people can change your life. She wasn't ready for that, but he couldn't see that at the time. Even when social media had started, he never had any interest. He saw her face clearly for the first time in many years. It was sad when she said it was a mistake. He'd never seen that, not until now. He wondered where she was. Chris Cornell sang on as he grabbed the gun and placed it on the desk.

In the final moment, he thought one thing. One thing. The final thing. Wow, it was the final thing… Even after thinking about going to Hell or where Nicole might be, it was the thing that itched at the back of his brain. Of course, that's not counting the bullet that would pass through in mere moments. Under other circumstances, he would have giggled at that bit of nonsense. He was no longer lost; maybe he would finally find peace.

As he lifted the gun, it felt heavy in his trembling hand, heavier than usual, but it could have just been the situation, and his mouth had grown very dry. For a moment he wanted to pause for a drink, but he only had a couple of minutes left to his song. Chris Cornell was baring his soul in the background and the sleepy man stared at the gun for another moment. As he slowly lifted it toward his mouth, a thought crossed his mind. *What is a lullaby?*

It made him pause for a moment. He thought to himself, a lullaby is a song to comfort children and help them fall asleep. A song? Yeah. And here was what confused him. How does anyone know if there is a song at all, or know the kind of song it is, if anyone who may have heard it could never share what it sounded like? Chris Cornell was almost finished with his song; the gun began to make its journey to its final home. Audioslave continued playing their song, and as it faded, the sleepless man played his song… He was surprised that he began to weep. And in the end,

he had regretted that he would never be able to

tell anyone that the lullaby had sounded utterly

beautiful…

A Fitting End:

They Call Them Death

The year is 2082, my name is Duncan Stills, and as of tonight, I am a senior council member of the World Leaders League (WLL). The purpose of the WLL is to keep our world safe from crime, war, or tyranny of any kind. A beautiful world, created by dedicated individuals that were willing to do anything that it took to create our utopia. As they say, you have to break a few eggs to make an omelet and truthfully, we'd broken a lot of eggs on the way to where we are now.

There are those, the older crowd; the Millennial-Golden Hairs consists of the first people born in the 21st century: the influencers, TikTok trenders, and meme creators. For all their bluster and need for attention and to be special,

they had no real talents, no real gifts that made
them extraordinary, no ability to make the world
better. Now they've grown old, and their vile,
ignorant ideas have aged as well as milk in the
sun. Those that ate laundry soap, choked on
spoonfuls of cinnamon, or dropped buckets of ice
on their heads are now mostly gone, but the few
that are left don't appreciate the haven that our
world has become. The antiquated theories and
ideas that they espoused are too weak for today.

It was that generation that almost ruined
America—or so my grandfather told me—and
the remainder of the world with it. Everything
triggered them, whatever being triggered really
was. Their opinions attempted to change basic
biology, and they could only lift phones to watch

the pain of others; they were too selfish to lift a single helping hand to help anyone. They would rather record a person being choked to death by police, being beaten on the street in a drunken fight, or even children being beaten by a parent. I read these things and see the multitude of videos online (Another thing they didn't realize is that that garbage, every bit of the videos and pictures, never goes away) and I cringe at those people and the things they did.

Yes, the pitiful lot they were, the advancements of the prior fifty years—from the early 1970s to the first ten years of the twenty-first century—had moved science, technology, and communications light years forward. Now everyone was too busy finding their own voice.

Why find their voice? So they could complain about how failure was never their fault.

My grandfather laid it out clearly for me as I grew up:

"White people complained that they had been marginalized by diversity initiatives. Black people complained that diversity initiatives did not sufficiently help their plight. And everyone else, well, they just wanted to be considered equal to the two big races."

In the end, that entire generation, regardless of color or race, spent more time looking for excuses than for ways to innovate and improve the world. Justice was imbued upon those with the funds to find representation that could twist the law enough to keep them from seeing the inside of a prison.

So how did we get to the world we have today, the veritable utopia that was created in the last fifty years? Two words: Blake Stills.

My grandfather started his career in the military in 2015. He spent ten years fighting all over the world, in the latter part of his time he was leading soldiers into dangerous locations and on clandestine missions. For the first eight years, he thanked God each morning for allowing him to live this life, for the soldiers he had brought home, and for the families of the soldiers who had lost their lives to allow our world to continue. He told me many times that he wanted to spend a lifetime in the military. But he cut his career short when he found that one moment that would change how he saw the world he had sworn to defend.

As a child, I heard the origin story of the WLL so many times, but I loved it—every single time my grandfather would take the time to tell it, he never wavered in his description. I've shared bits and pieces of it over the years, so it just seems right to share it all here. And no better time than now; I have a while before my first WLL meeting as a member!

One night, my grandfather was the sergeant over the staff duty desk. This was a twenty- four-hour assignment where he kept an eye and ear out for any trouble. He'd done this many times

over the course of his career. A typical weekend
would see him contacting commanders for drunk
soldiers that chose to fight or drive. On this night,
though, he was called to the home of the Alpha
Company commander's home. Trust me when I
say, I've never forgotten how my grandfather
described the scene. His voice as he told the story
was almost dead, which made sense, as this was
the night he decided to end his military career:

"I walked into this stunning home. Officers
really lived well. But inside, it was smelly and
filthy. Dogs were barking from somewhere
within the home, which was why dog feces
covered the floor. Along with the two MPs that
had entered the home with me, we walked past
garbage, boxes of old food, broken furniture. We

turned a corner into a crowded, filthy kitchen. This was where a battered woman sat on the floor, crumbled, defeated, and bloody. A thin, brunette woman who looked as if she had been a cheerleader or beauty queen in high school, but the years—and, apparently, her husband—had not treated her well. I was taken aback when she looked up at me, desperation and sadness in her eyes. She appeared to no longer have the ability nor care to find anger; the captain's wife was in sheer survival mode, and she looked like she'd been there for a long time.

"One of the MPs started to call for a rescue unit for an injured woman, but I asked him to delay for a moment, to go to his vehicle and get a first aid kit until I said differently. The MP stared for a moment, then ran to his vehicle. We waited until he returned to continue. He squatted down and began to speak to the battered woman, asking what had happened and who had done this. The second MP and I walked deeper into the home. From upstairs, I heard children, maybe two or three, crying and calling for their mother. She was on the floor of the kitchen, and this really started to piss me off. We looked left, right, and up the stairs, and the garbage and filth seemed to have no end.

"Eventually, we found Captain Reynolds. He was a cocky, thin, boisterous man. I was a platoon sergeant in Bravo Company. I'd seen Captain Reynolds around and had spoken to some of his NCOs (Non-commissioned Officers);

he was not well liked by anyone. A known heavy drinker, smoker, and loudmouth. He spoke down to anyone below his grade; he thought his rank gave him the right to do so. So, this MP and I walked into an office that seemed to be the only place he kept clean. I've never forgotten that. His family's living quarters were completely trashed, and there was his little sanctuary full of stupid models and trinkets of vehicles he'd never ridden in and wars he'd never fought. Reynolds had a drink in his right hand and was scrolling through Pornhub with his left. I immediately knew two things: he'd heard us enter and was ignoring us as a power play, and he thought he was in charge. I cleared my throat, and he spun his desk chair to stare at us. We observed that his knuckles were covered in the beauty queen's blood, and they appeared to have been used very violently.

"And just what the fuck do you two want, Sergeant?" the asshole said as if he'd done nothing wrong. He sneered, spit in our general direction, and spun around to stare at his porn again.

"I'm not sure if it was the way he slurred his words, his smell and appearance, or if I had just seen enough. I'd done everything right my entire career. I overlooked shitty leaders and power-hungry soldiers, and at that very moment, I was done. I looked to the MP and merely said, 'Close the door.' He had a wary look, but did what I said. I began to walk toward the drunken man, and in one fluid motion, as the door clicked, I grabbed the man's drink and used the glass to get his attention. By the time the MP grabbed me, I had given Reynolds three solid reasons to re-think his life. (Sorry to interrupt, but my grandfather always laughed at that, and he never really laughed at anything.)

"At that point, I cleared my head and thought through everything ahead of me if I did not choose my words wisely. I spoke slowly and clearly. I told Reynolds that if he laid another hand on his wife, I would visit him with no MP to stop me from shoving his glass up his pompous ass. There would be no more hiding what he was doing. I reminded him that it was unbecoming of an officer to beat on his wife. I asked him if he understood, and through his bloody, blackened eyes, I knew he understood that I meant to injure him permanently if I came back here. As I turned to walk out, I looked back one last time and told him to clean the place up.

"As we walked to the front, I asked the MP that was helping Mrs. Reynolds to call rescue for her and child services for the children upstairs now. As rescue and social services arrived and took over the scene, I took a moment to speak to the two young men that had entered with me, and we decided that my visit and talk with the fine Captain Reynolds was to remain off the record— Mrs. Reynolds was taken to the hospital for a bad fall in her home. The Reynolds children would sleep in a clean and warm bed, as their father was indisposed, and their mother would pick them up in the morning. I remember thinking that she would go right back home as soon as she got her children; it turned my stomach to know that. As for Captain Reynolds, he was not seen by the ambulance staff and did not go to the hospital that night.

"A lot changed in me that night. I discovered there's no justice for those that can't afford to complain or speak out. With my having smacked Reynolds around and seeing immediate results, the embers began to burn for the beginning of what would become the WLL. I thought that if people were willing to step up, to act when it was needed, and to stop making legality an issue of wealth, power, and privilege, then we could move forward. Forward meaning that the willingness to do the right thing when it's necessary was exactly what you would do. Sure, it was just a thread of an idea really, but a thread can hold together a beautiful suit if you work with it enough. A lot needed to be done, and it would shift over time. But yes, that's where it began."

I would stand up and clap each time he told that story. Never did he change it to make himself sound like a hero or add any other embellishment. He always looked serene after finishing the story. Recalling those moments made him young again, like the whole trip was ahead of him once again, and I knew that he would not have changed anything. Not one moment.

So, the very next day my grandfather would

begin shifting to leave the military. Once he made up his mind, there was no going back. That thread had started making the suit he would wear for the remainder of his life. He had done just over ten years, and he could leave in the next six months. He put in his paperwork, and he used all his connections from all his travels during his military service. He started by sending out feelers for his vision of the future to those people that he knew he could trust. Whether or not they chose to follow his lead, they would never betray his trust; integrity was key. At this time, he was single, and he had saved a meat of his leave. This allowed him several months to keep finding his contacts and people he felt would do what needed to be done, and to continue getting paid while finding his footing outside of the military. During the time he was on terminal leave, he immediately enrolled in college and would major in law with a minor in political science. He met my grandmother sometime in the next couple years.

In just four years, he finished with a law degree. By going every available semester year-round, he quickly achieved his first goal. He passed the bar on his first try and hung his shingle in a small town in North Carolina. What pushed him through school was the image of Captain Reynolds sneering and spitting in his direction. He thought about what he felt was too much injustice in the world, and he used his time in school and in his work to continue making his connections with like-minded people: the leaders of tomorrow, people not afraid to start making waves right away. He would say these men and women were fearless; they clearly saw the vision and made it a living thing.

His first political office was as state representative for his district in North Carolina. His goals were always present in his mind: he would spend no more than two years in any position. He was a rolling stone. "Blake Stills is a motivated man!" *USA Today* had made that statement when he made his successful run at the presidency. Of course, along the way came my father. My grandfather was an attentive father, but his family knew that they came second to his burgeoning career. He had to stay focused. My father would speak of him as a good man, but not a fun dad. It bothered me that he felt that way. My grandfather was changing the world, playing catch should not have been high on the totem pole.

As the first independent governor of North Carolina, Blake Stills had made strides to advance police weaponry, allowing individuals to make a choice on whether they would carry a child to term or not, and he adjusted the justice system to allow for swifter sentencing and punishment. Along with updates to the state court system, he introduced a bill to limit the number of appeals a criminal could introduce, thereby freeing up the court for new cases. This became standard across the country very quickly. The one flaw in his governing, according to the

Christians, was that he had no need for religion in regard to politics and policies. Many before, knowing nothing of God, had played the game, calling themselves Christians just to appeal to that group of voters. My grandfather never felt any need to pretend. He told me many times that politicians who leaned on God or religion were just as weak-minded as those people that believed a book over science, technology, and common sense. What he knew was how to lead. He made no qualms about not being a nice guy or religious. It became obvious that he attracted voters with his rhetoric. Grandfather projected strength, confidence, and believability. He was not a politician, he was a man that wanted to change the world. It was actually one of his first campaign slogans: "A Vote for Stills Will Change Our State and Our World."

Both Democrats and Republicans wanted him when whispers became screams that this man, a former enlisted man and lawyer, would soon be president. Here, again, Blake Stills would shun the powers that be and run for the party that he founded: the Leader's League. His platform was clear and undeniably what people wanted, and his speeches could make even the most unapologetically hated rivals stand to cheer. He did not mince words or ride the fence. He spoke his truth. He spoke the country's and even the world's truth. And when he said he would change things, that he had a plan to make our country and our world a better place for all law-abiding people, one thing was completely clear—the people took notice and believed him.

Granddad had agreed to debate the incumbent and the other party's top candidate. They thought they had a chance to show him up: he was younger, less experienced, and they were going to embarrass him on a grand stage. It was an interesting plan…until Granddad folded them like laundry. He was ready. Policy, laws, plans, and more. He was so utterly prepared for the debate that it was over after only two questions. But it continued and got worse for the other candidates. The moderators allowed one minute for closing comments, and my grandfather let them have it.

"I am not a politician. I cannot and will not

ever be bought, unlike the two individuals beside me. Their ideas are as antiquated as their policies. Our country needs change. Not tomorrow, but now! As your next president, I will implement changes as soon as I arrive. I will make sense of the mess that has been made by the individuals that have sold you out for decades. I am not a Republican nor a Democrat, and I'm definitely not dumb. Day one, the *For Sale* sign comes off the White House's front door. On day two, I'll push for new changes in the countries that we have treaties with. We will no longer be the world's doormat. And after that will come the big changes. The world will once again acknowledge us as the top of the food chain. Thank you."

He walked from the stage that night and had

not only won the debate; America knew that he would be their next president. All that was left was the election. Once he had indeed won, it was time to get to work. He had promised to hit the ground running, so as he was preparing to take his oath of office, President Stills began reaching out to his military friends, his law school friends both in and outside of the United States, and other politicians the world over that had caught his attention in his last few years. What the world was not yet aware of, but something that would quickly become very clear, was that he had assembled a very powerful network. My grandfather moved swiftly to change the landscape of the world. He would bring real justice, true peace, and his worldwide network of cohesive leaders together to unite the world. Those that didn't know Granddad thought he might be a mean or overbearing man, but he did not lead with an iron fist or shout orders to others. He had a clear vision and surrounded himself with those that could create that vision with him. He never would have been comfortable watching others build his vision without being there; rather, he did his best to be hands-on with kid gloves. And with that single vision amongst his staff, things began to move quickly.

Within one year, he had changed the law so that all prisons would be emptied. To the younger ones that read this, you may ask what a prison was, or if they ever really existed. Yes, they existed. Their purpose was to cage criminals, and they were places of violence, disease, and rape. With the liberties that started taking place in the mid-20s such as trans prisoners getting to choose to be in a facility of their affirmed gender and big-name criminals never seeing the inside of the cells that should have held them, it all had become a circus run by gangs. So, what Granddad did to empty those cells surprised everyone.

Offenders of any kind were all executed at the exact same time the world over. No appeal, no lawyer, no excuses. Those on probation or home arrest found themselves on the business end of that as well. It was over just like that. Offenders that were minors, though, were released after witnessing the executions of all the others. They watched as a warning, their *one* warning. Upon release, they were labeled via microchip as prior offenders. Any subsequent offenses meant immediate termination of that individual. The problem with this process was how to find someone willing to take action on these offenders immediately. My grandfather and his partners, with the WLL still a few years away, had already thought of that.

Now, some of you might remember that this was when my grandfather instituted the Reaper Program. Individuals that became Reapers would later be known simply as Deaths. Early in the project, the Deaths were all current or former soldiers. Soldiers were chosen for this because they had killed as a job, and this was just an extension of that power. For those that don't know their history, the Reapers travelled through the entire prison system in one night, including hospitals where violent offenders resided. From murderers and pedophiles to forgers and drunks, all were slaughtered. Not sparing anyone was an important part of kicking off the WLL. The world over, leaders were unified and not backing down. It was that unity that pushed the WLL forward. My grandfather and the other world leaders that saw his vision were truly reshaping and changing the world. They offered the genuinely good people of the world the ability to sleep peacefully, enjoy walking in the evening, and not having to worry about their kids playing outside.

Sure, this first-time experiment with the Reapers was surprising and scary to the general public, but it set a very strong precedent. Granddad always made it clear that initially there was a bit of a pushback. It was later determined that it was the prisoners' families that pushed back. Some of them tried to sue the government, and there were protests. But the Reapers put a quick stop to those protests; no one dared break the law after what they had seen. The morning after the initial extermination had been done, my grandfather would say that "it was a very positive and necessary step in the fight on crime and the advancement of humankind."

As for the lawsuits, he quickly squashed those; again, it was a unified front worldwide with my grandfather as the face. He stated to the American public (and had form letters sent to all the survivors of the deceased.) that there would be no settlements, there would be no backing down from what had happened, and if anyone decided to break any laws stating their opinions, they would soon be meeting up with their criminal family members. No weakness would be shown by his administration, law enforcement, or the Reapers.

Okay, here's a bragging moment for me that not many people know: my grandfather confided in me that early on, he had gladly been a Reaper on several occasions. He had been in on the initial prisoner extermination. As a soldier and man, he had never liked criminals of any sort. Getting on the wrong side of the law had no excuse. My granddad had instilled that in me from my first steps. Law and order made us safe and advanced us as a society.

Again, my grandfather was a married man at this time, and my father had come along a few years earlier. My father told me he grew up in a happy home; my grandmother was doting, and my grandfather was good to him. But my father was not like him—or me, for that matter— and he wanted nothing to do with politics or the WLL. My father was an academic and would become a law professor. The practice of law was more policies and contracts as criminals had all but disappeared. So, teaching during that time was good as things were changing rapidly. My granddad loved my dad, but they were so different. Granddad had been an athlete and influential in groups for much of his life. My dad, on the other hand, was a quiet and subdued man that kept to himself. He was not "outstanding"— at least that's what my grandfather had told me.

My grandfather took an interest in me because he felt that I was, indeed, outstanding. I was exceptionally bright, athletic, and liked amongst my peers. I graduated first in my class and took a football scholarship to college. I loved football and could have pursued a professional career, but I jumped into the "family business" as soon as I graduated college. Being a Stills did not automatically put me in the WLL; I worked hard for that. But like my grandfather, I love justice. I wanted to make a mark in government. Having earned a degree in civics and policy, I started as an advocate for low-income individuals. I moved much like my grandfather—no more than two years anywhere. Moving up in responsibility and pushing myself to be better. One of the last times I spoke with Granddad, he told me that I had become the outstanding individual that could move the world forward; he said he wished he could see what I would become…

So, back to the week after all prisoners had been eradicated. President Stills encouraged—rather strongly—local jails to do the same. He even offered to send help if the local jailers weren't up to doing the job. On the podium, he would hug my father and speak with all the fire of a Southern Baptist preacher trying to get money. "The Reaper program was started to make your children safe and to make my son safe. I have commitments from over eighty percent of the current United Nations to leave that ancient organization and start the World Leaders League."

That was it! On that day, November 16, 2043, my grandfather uttered the name of the WLL for the first time. He was the most powerful man in the world, and his friends were just as powerful in each of their own countries, but everyone followed my grandfather's lead. Another two years passed; the Reaper Program was becoming quite popular. It was at this time that people officially called them Deaths. It was still known who the Reapers were; if you knew one, you hoped it would never be in a business way.

President Stills became known for his passion for justice for all people and making the ridiculous in law a thing of the past, but more on that later. What my grandfather really did in that first presidency was change the world. He changed how things were done.

His changes were all about the justice system, the military, and bringing equality to the masses.

As I sit here and write this, I wonder, is there anyone that doesn't know what changed? There can't be, I know, but this is for posterity's sake. So, I'll start… The justice system changed in the following ways:

1. Within five years, all law enforcement was a thing of the past. No more criminal courts or lawyers, and no police force. When he first suggested it, people thought he was crazy, but it worked so well out of the box that people couldn't deny the effectiveness.

2. The military was done within another five years. All soldiers were released from their enlistments and contracts. The interesting part was that all the countries that had entered the WLL did the same thing. The world leaders were all friendly and had been in discussions about the way to go about this. President Stills said that the United States would lead the way. When they did, the world followed.

3. Equality. It was the hardest to change because

that bit had been so ingrained. Worldwide, there were people that thought they deserved to be respected because of their color, name, or money. People wanted to be victims; they wanted an excuse to be angry. Individuals that complained about being held down due to sexual orientation, race, sexual identity, and all the other victim mentalities would be quieted. The WLL made changes to stop both the superiority and victim groups from having an excuse, but it took another solid five years of work on all levels.

And how was it all accomplished? The Reaper Program. After the initial Reaper sweep of the prisons, the program would go through several evolutions. The first major change came after the militaries of the world were dissolved. The leaders didn't want to use ex-military in this role on a continuing basis; they had done enough service to the government. What they did was find suitable employment for the former soldiers. The world governments started peeling back the layers of fat on their budgets. All the career politicians were made to leave. During his second term, the president made it clear that they would leave office the same way they came into office. Those politicians thought they would leave with all their ill-gotten money from under-the-table deals, lobbyists, and illegal deals; unfortunately for them, they were all offered options. Keep your money, and your official last will and testament will donate it all back to the government and leave your family nothing. And you die that night. End of your term.

Or leave it all and live a long, simple life. Self-preservation kicked in for most of them. There were always those that thought they knew an angle, but the WLL left no angles.

My grandfather, laughing his rough old man's laugh, told me about one senator that told him to go fuck himself, that he would leave with what he had, and if my grandfather didn't like it, then the senator's bodyguard would make it clear to him. So this senator motioned to his bodyguard to approach the president. It was crazy: this old fucker had taken money hand over fist for decades from "special interest" groups and sponsors, and now he wanted to strong-arm the president of the United

States? It was, from the description, one hell of a few minutes.

My grandfather motioned his Secret Service men to stand down. The bodyguard, 6' 4" and 250 pounds, was an intimidating man. He had short dark hair and was maybe 30 years old; by his gait, my grandfather knew the man had been military. A muscular arm reached toward the president, but my grandfather, never one to panic or fold, stood his ground.

Here's a fun fact: My grandfather had a photographic memory for two things— faces and names. When he met you once, he knew you always. And he treated everyone around him with respect; until, of course, they showed they no longer deserved that respect. If he met a soldier, bodyguard, or Secret Service member (any security, really; they were the truly dangerous ones in the room), he made a point to greet them and ask a personal question each subsequent time he saw them. Now back to your regularly scheduled program.

So, this senator has a shit-eating grin as his bodyguard approached my grandfather. What that senator, the Secret Service covering my grandfather, and any others in the room didn't know was that my grandfather had crossed paths with this man long ago. The bodyguard had raised a muscular arm with one goal: to greet my grandfather. His open hand was met by my grandfather's. They shook hands, shared a smile, and a small nod from my grandfather prompted the man into action.

Before the other men in the room could react, the man turned and shot a round, center mass, at the confused and no longer smiling senator. The man died moments after thinking he was the smartest man in the room.

"How have you been, Phillip? And your father?"

"We've been excellent, sir. It's a pleasure to see you again." The bodyguard holstered his weapon, turned in a military fashion, and walked out of the room.

That had truly been my grandfather's superpower: he was always the smartest man in the room. Anything you knew, he knew a bit more about it. The best part of this superpower was that he never showed his hand till it was time. He made others feel powerful until it was time to show them who was really in power.

I personally thought it was for the surprised look on the losers' faces. There was nothing like seeing a shit-eating grin turn into a *What the fuck just happened?* look.

That incident sped along, ridding the world of unnecessary government officials. Many in the world loved that aspect of the changes; especially the people that cried to defund police and government to help move their agendas forward. Little did those people know what would come next.

President Stills was motivated to push the

WLL's mission forward. Upon the world governments peeling back the layers, the first official iteration of the World Leaders League consisted of 30 world leaders. President Stills was made the first ever WLL leader, not because he was from the United States, former military, a bully, white, or any other reason the crying Millennial Golden-Hairs' generation would push as reasons that he had become the leader. No, he was made the leader because he had the vision to begin this journey and a vision for the future that others could not yet see. When the leaders would meet, it was obvious that he was filled with ideas and a very clear vision of what needed to happen, where it needed to happen, and how they all would make it happen. He knew and always acknowledged that he could not do this alone: the WLL, from the beginning, was for many leaders, not just one dictator. That's what many people thought, but my grandfather never thought any one person should have all the power. They were all leaders for a reason.

It was during college that my grandfather met my grandmother. Jillian Bell was a teacher in the area; they met at a mutual friend's gathering. They dated for a short time and would marry; in the next two years, they would welcome my father. My father, born of opportunity, would grow up very close to my grandmother. They both stayed very much behind the scenes.

As my grandfather ascended to power, his family was rather low on his list of priorities.

Don't get me wrong, he treated them well, but changing the world became his number one priority. He lived that mission day after day and on into decades. There was never any anger or animosity; again, my grandfather was building a new world. New powers that would change how justice, servitude, and government ran the world. After his terms as president and league leader, a full twenty years later, my grandfather would walk away from service. The world had changed forever. He and my grandmother would spend their golden years getting to know one another again. They truly loved each other, and she spent her final minutes in his arms.

My parents, though, were not so happy together. It was always a source of bother for my grandparents. After their divorce, I chose to stay with my grandparents. My father was always teaching, and my mother simply enjoyed trying to stay young and drunk with her new boy toys. It was best for me to stay where I had some stability. But that's enough of my family tree.

My grandfather spent hours upon hours telling me his tales and the importance of service to my country. So yes, I chose service. I wanted to be like my grandfather. I have worked to be his shadow, not a clone. My grandfather always told me to be my own man. Choose to do right but do it your way. I kept all his tips, tricks, and stories very close to my chest.

During the final years of the first League leaders, the Reaper Program continued to evolve.

Many of the current Reapers were the original lot that had followed the soldiers. But they were all looking to walk away now, to begin new lives. One of my grandfather's final decrees as league leader was to declare that becoming a Reaper would be done by secret lot. Anyone could request the opportunity, but only certain ones would ever be chosen.

A battery of questions was developed from what all the world leaders would decide was needed of a Reaper. The questions were behavior based, mental evaluations, and social adeptness. This next round of Reapers was a big step toward the brutality that was to come.

The lack of local and state government scared some people that could not see the vision of the leaders. But it was straightforward, there were no more government jobs (no military or civilian government). Locally, communities recognized a spokesperson; the only oversight for those individuals were Reapers. And to keep them honest, they did not know who was watching them. The WLL found that fear of death was a great cure for crooked leaders.

That was the thing: only the League knew who the Reapers were, where they were hidden, and what methods they would use to bring justice. So anywhere you were, any time you stepped out of line, there was a possibility that someone was watching. After the identities of the Reapers became secret, there were protests about those individuals having free reign and no oversight.

Sure, people were free to protest, but you didn't dare destroy property or do anything that could be seen as illegal in the eyes of the Reapers. The second- generation Reapers took to executing those that stepped out of line for any infractions.

It's so strange how quickly people fall in line when an unknown entity could be watching them at any time. It started with a clear vision, using common sense and punishing those that choose not to follow the rules. There was leeway for the Reapers, but most found that killing offenders set a tone.

It took maybe three years before crime had all but disappeared. It was quite simple: You fuck up in any way, you die. No second chances, no do-overs. It was said that if you begged for your life, the Reaper took more time to finish you. Whether that was true or not, no one really wanted to know.

As a decade passed, the next group of Reapers began to be ushered into their calling. With all criminals having been eradicated, many that were caught in the justice system saw this as a do-over. The gist was that criminals made the perfect Reapers. Many of the mentally ill ones had a twisted but absolute vision of justice. It was all about not having a conscience to guide them. This was what the leaders had wanted from the beginning. These types of individuals were perfect machines for what needed to be done.

Anonymity in the ranks of the Reapers made them harder to see coming. Within three years of the beginning of the fourth generation, the name

Reapers was completely gone. "Death" simply meant that it was something you didn't see coming for you and gave you no choice. Plus, those that chose not to work within the constraints of the law and common sense were often left displayed in a very public manner.

Examples were what made those skirting the law stop what they were doing. The Deaths brought a sense of freedom to those in the world that had feared going out at night, being assaulted in public, rising prices from thievery, and any type of lawlessness.

The further from a dystopian society that the early twenty-first century had become—that had been part of life in that time—the less examples hung in the middle of town. The less the Deaths had to work.

There are always those that push, but pushing was not smart. Ever.

The ones that had the hardest time were the Deaths that worked near schools. Sure, corporal punishment was brought back for the kids. For a bit, it did change things. But the kids eventually thought that their actions were above reproach. Only that first group, all those years ago, got one extra chance. Now came the hard work. When these teens or younger children acted out, they took a few lashes and laughed in the faces of the school administrators giving out the punishment. This latest generation of Reapers...they would change that.

The first batch of executed students were

found countrywide on an April morning in 2073. Although their identities were unknown by others, the Reapers could find one another, on a secure network where they would get paid. They signed in with the lottery number with which they had applied to the program and the password they had established. They claimed their funds, which were placed into their account and then downloaded by them via an encrypted network. The one other thing that was provided was a secure chat function. It had been added during the second generation; the Reapers could coordinate their efforts to make the maximum impact.

In late winter of 2073, the Reapers had grown wary of the disrespect of the students. The conversations started with suggestions of punishing the parents or possibly the school personnel that were not helping the children see the importance of behaving. Soon, the newer Reapers started another conversation that resulted in finding examples worldwide of students that continued to push. One thing became apparent to everyone amongst the Reapers: they had never had the heart to kill children. Before now.

Kids were not fully developed mentally, and they made rash choices; they were just kids. One of the Reapers made the case with a brilliant example.

"Women were not allowed in combat for centuries. Why? Because a man would pause if he were faced with killing a female soldier. Or, even worse, were a woman to be the soldier beside you, would you make the decision to treat her like any other soldier or would you try to protect her? When women were thrown into combat, many male soldiers worldwide found that they paused, and the females did not. What the Reapers need to do is stop thinking of these poorly mannered children as weak. We need to stop the attitudes, actions, and the free feeling of being able to just get a few hits with a board or switch. I propose that we all find a local student, one that has been a constant problem. Will people be upset? Yes. Do we care? No. We can't care, and we can't hesitate. If we hesitate here, we'll lose the next generation. Everything that the WLL and the Reapers have worked toward for decades will go backward. We'll lose the momentum that the Reapers before us created. We must act now. As a Reaper, I know that the vision of the League was for us to make society better for everyone. What say you all?"

It hung there for hours. No one wanted to be the first to reply. This was a tough one. Then it happened. "I completely agree, we must act now or lose momentum." After that, it was like a flood.

It was an overwhelmingly positive vote. The Reapers worked in stealth, as always. They picked the worst of the worst students. Age was not the problem; it was their attitudes, their offenses, the number of repeat offenses, and their unwillingness to be helped. Those chosen had been offered chances over and over. And they refused to change their ways. So, they had unwittingly volunteered to be part of *Operation Save the Generation.*

All these children were hung by meat hooks through their shoulders. They were tortured for hours—this was done so that the Reapers would never pause again. At a moment's notice, a Reaper would act in the best interest of society. They had to hear the children's screams and their begging at least once. All of them heard the screams for hours; it wasn't widely spoken about in the online conversations, but those that did speak shared very dark and twisted tales. These Reapers were some of our criminals, but they did their jobs. And it was all that mattered.

Early in the night, the students that had been chosen were taken from their homes in an expedient manner. As the sun came close to rising, the students were finally put out of their misery.

Printed signs were hung around their necks:

"The disrespect ends with me. The Reapers will no longer accept the poor attitudes and illicit actions of ANY child. If a child chooses to step out of line, they are asking for adult punishment.

*-   **Your Reapers**"*

There was immediate outrage; some parents became the next individuals to meet with a Reaper. Those older ones saw it as a step in the right direction. Killing children— that had made the world sit up and take notice. No more illegal activity would be tolerated at any level. Everyone would be held to a standard. It was clear that good people and a nice clean world were where we were now going. There were no political shenanigans, no favors to be done. Everyone was working together. There were no wars, no borders, and people worked to build one another up. This new generation of people were strong because they knew no enemies, no borders, no limits. It was a world that held a tangible beauty.

It had all changed. My grandfather's vision had come to life. The last part was getting rid of bad attitudes before they began. The beginning of the changes could not possibly have wholly predicted what was happening now. But here it was.

Orwell, for all his clear visions of *1984*, couldn't have predicted this world that my grandfather had envisioned and created, and that I now keep moving forward. I was appointed as the League leader just last week. Coming in as the leader of the WLL was an outstanding feat, but Granddad had always said that I was outstanding. All the books of the early twentieth century saw the future as dystopian. But my grandfather had made the world a beautiful place.

After finishing high school and before I went on to play football, I applied for a job. My wish had always been to be a Reaper. I was accepted on my first try. I was in my early twenties and needed to make my own way. Being a Reaper gave me anonymity to move along in my career and not be compared to my grandfather. I had been a Reaper for two years when the April 2073 events took place.

After I sent the message about women in combat and the suggestion about the children to my fellow Reapers, I moved us into a virtually crime-free world. I gave up my chair as a Death two months ago. We still find new ways to improve the world. The League voted to make all currency virtual. People still work and earn. No one pays taxes to the government. All retirements are privatized. The economy is steady, no inflation, and poverty is over.

In this new world, everyone pitches in. If you want to live off the grid, you will not live off society's tit. In the end, there is no dystopia waiting because we acted. We did not accept what the world had become. We knew how to make the changes, and we had the guts to do it.

The League leaders stopped allowing the patients to run the asylum. To state it plainly, do things that make sense. You protest, protest peacefully. You want to be something other than your birth sex, don't complain if no one wants to play along with you. If society does something you don't like, simply ask why, then wait and listen.

That had become society's tragic flaw. Everyone thought that their opinion mattered and that everyone else was wrong if they thought otherwise. *Pansies*, my grandfather had called them. Not in an effeminate way, but just to say that they were weak-minded. Sheep, followers that thought they were leaders. Again, my grandfather knew that to lead you needed to know how to follow, and that everyone should have an opinion, but not every opinion was correct.

In this new world run by Deaths, you could still speak freely, but you didn't make a spectacle of yourself. Don't push your agendas if they are nonsensical; unpopular but peaceful demonstrations were always acceptable. Deaths had made the world simple. It had always been the ones that were living in this world that would from time to time make it difficult again.

As I am preparing to address the other leaders, I look up at the portrait of my grandfather. The founder of the world as we know it, the man had truly been a genius. At the beginning, many called him a fascist. A dictator. Many people thought of him as a bad man. But he liked all people the same way, if they were law abiding. You could be any color, religion, or sex and you got the respect from him that you gave. Always.

The citizens that wanted to survive and thrive in the world thought of him as a liberator. My grandfather, for his part, did not ever consider himself special. He was not into anyone blindly following him or his platform. His favorite statement to those that called him a savior:

"Don't be silly! I'm a man. Just like other men, and I make mistakes, and I am a continual learner. I implore you to read, learn about the issues at hand, take care of those around you, and please be continual learners yourselves. In the end, our future depends on our getting along with one another and making our society one that we want to exist and live in and raise our children."

Tears roll down my cheeks; this man was my hero. He literally changed the world for the better. A person that was a hero to so many, my personal hero had spent so much time with me. Teaching me about leadership, love, and becoming a man. I continue walking to my office, my suit is pressed. It's a grey suit, a white shirt, and blue and green striped tie; they won't be able to see my black patent leather wingtip shoes, but I wear them as well. My grandfather had always told me to be 100% dressed and prepared for every meeting and speech. I was prepared. I was made the leader of the League. Men all over the world would be looking to me for my ideas and my leadership.

The entire time, all the words and actions that

the man had shared with me had set me up to one day be a leader just like him. My father had never wanted this. He wanted to stay as far away from service as possible. My grandfather loved him, but they couldn't see eye to eye on anything. Still, there was no animosity, just a different view on life.

As a professor of law, my father was an extremely opinionated and knowledgeable man. But some of his ideas were antiquated by the day's standards. Still, my grandfather always loved his son.

I sit down and press my suit jacket flat and look for loose threads or any unsightly fuzz; I think to myself and glance over my notes. I'm prepared to begin. Only the leaders have access to this online meeting. This will be my first official address to the entire body.

It's just minutes from beginning, I breathe. It's important to control your breathing; when you control that, you control yourself. A person in complete control of themselves can control others around him. If you can't control yourself, how can you ever control anyone around you? Yes, my grandfather. So much wisdom—Goddamn, I miss him.

A minute away, I'm ready. The camera is not yet on, all the other leaders have their cameras off as well. It's an old tradition: no cameras or microphones before meeting time.

Forty-five seconds; all of this, my life and

everything about it—I look back. As a Death, I had experienced so many feelings. Some nights were exhilarating. Other nights I did not want to do what needed to be done. But Death does not take a night off and neither did I.

Thirty seconds; it was a cold January night. I knew the assignment. It was in my vicinity, and thus, my responsibility. By this time, Deaths could access any building, home, or office. Everything used electronic locks. I used my all-access lock card. I saw the green light; no noise, just a light.

Fifteen seconds; I walked into the office as the man sat quietly staring out the window. A glass of bourbon in one hand and a pipe in his mouth, the man was humming a tune from an old 2040s song.

Ten seconds; I walked quietly up to the smoking man. The ticket was called in because this man had been privately teaching subversive ideas, long-gone rules, and theories to his students. The man was aware of his responsibilities as a teacher of the next generation. He should have stayed the course. He knew his assignment but chose not to follow the rules.

Five seconds; I clear my throat, and the man turns to face me. And he says the last word he would ever utter.

"Son?"

Three seconds; I used a straight-edged razor. I stood above him, and as he looked up at me, he left his neck completely exposed. I cut my father's throat and watched him bleed out. As the blood was running down his chest, he would attempt to speak, a desperate look on his face as I dragged him outside to leave the mark of Death. I remember clearing my throat; I was a bit choked up (if I'm being honest) remembering how proud my grandfather had been when he saw that his own son had been taken by his grandson. Even now, I know he created this world for me. And I must continue his vision.

Two. One.

"Good evening, League leaders. You know me. I'm proud to sign on today as our leader. We move forward into a utopia that no one…no one could have ever predicted. And we few will lead the charge into an even greater future…"

Epilogue:

Being the leader, I feel that the emphasis given by protestors on peaceful resolutions is quite interesting. By definition, protesting or civil disobedience was meant to bring change, but they don't see that the sacrifices made by the world leadership and the Reapers actually made change. They judge us for eradicating criminals. Yet, they prosper from our work. They are saddened by the examples made by eliminating some very poorly mannered children.

It's always children. You can kill a million men and women, but harm a hair on a child's head and you're a monster. It's quite ridiculous, but thus it is the life of a complainer, or protestor, whichever you call them is the same. Don't get what you want, write posters, stand on the sidewalk, chant and yell. Do what you want but let us govern. Let us protect you.

The meeting had ended hours ago; it went very well. Being the leader weighs heavy on a man and you can't lose focus for even a moment. Our world is a utopia. The average person thinks our methods were a bit heavy-handed; I get it. My grandfather and his allies were tough men. But to continue our ascension to betterment, we must be as hard-hearted as those men. If you see wrong, you act.

A subtle difference is people don't watch wrong just occur; they put down their phones and they help. They know that a Reaper will find them just as culpable of the wrongdoing for recording it.

Our principles were forced to change. Our very existence is based on a truth we tell ourselves, and that is: we are always free to make a choice, but we must prepare to face real consequences for those choices. It's a beautiful world if your choices accept our reality.

About the Author:

Juan grew up in San Augustine, TX and found his love for writing and acting at a young age. He attended college on theater scholarships. Upon leaving school early, he joined the Army from 1995-1999. After leaving the Army, he worked for the government until 2016. During that time, he worked on several television programs, movies, and on stage. In 2020, Juan published a children's book, "We're All Broken". Having been married for almost 30 years, Juan and his wife have two adult children. They live in Washington State.

www.ingramcontent.com/pod-product-compliance
Lightning Source LLC
Chambersburg PA
CBHW071458110726
47908CB00003B/652